TO THE EDGE
OF THE ABYSS

THOMAS M. DISCH is one of the finest young science fiction writers today.

These seventeen highly imaginative stories will fascinate both the science fiction buff and the connoisseur of flawless craftsmanship, memorable characters, and the unexpected in the short story.

Other SIGNET Science Fiction Titles You Will Enjoy

☐ **DRIFTGLASS Ten Tales of Speculative Fiction by Samuel R. Delany.** Rooted in the present, projected into the future, this is a highly imaginative collection of tales by one of science fiction's most original authors. (#Q4834—95¢)

☐ **DOWN IN THE BLACK GANG by Philip José Farmer.** An action-filled collection of seven stories and a novelette by a man who has had a revolutionary impact on the science fiction scene.
(#T4805—75¢)

☐ **GALAXIES LIKE GRAINS OF SAND by Brian Aldiss.** An exciting chronicle of eight distant tomorrows—each another step forward into the future reaches of time and space.
(#T4781—75¢)

☐ **DO ANDROIDS DREAM OF ELECTRIC SHEEP? by Philip K. Dick.** An original and satirically funny tale by one of science fiction's most original authors, this book is about Rick Decard, a cop with an unusual beat and an unusual assignment—to kill six androids. (#T4758—75¢)

THE NEW AMERICAN LIBRARY, INC.
P.O. Box 999, Bergenfield, New Jersey 07621

Please send me the SIGNET BOOKS I have checked above. I am enclosing $_____(check or money order—no currency or C.O.D.'s). Please include the list price plus 15¢ a copy to cover mailing costs.

Name_____

Address_____

City_____State_____Zip Code_____
Allow at least 3 weeks for delivery

FUN WITH YOUR
• NEW HEAD

By Thomas M. Disch

A SIGNET BOOK from
NEW AMERICAN LIBRARY
TIMES MIRROR

COPYRIGHT © 1968 BY THOMAS M. DISCH

All rights reserved. For information address
Doubleday & Company, Inc., 277 Park Avenue,
New York, New York 10017.

Library of Congress Catalog Card Number: 72-132503

"The Roaches," copyright © 1965 by Bruce-Royal Publishing Co. First published in *Escapade*, October 1965.

"Come to Venus Melancholy," copyright © 1965 by Mercury Press, Inc. First published in *The Magazine of Fantasy and Science Fiction*, November 1965.

"Linda and Daniel and Spike," copyright © 1968 by Thomas M. Disch.

"Descending," copyright © 1964 by Ziff-Davis Publishing Company. First published in *Fantastic*, July 1964.

"Nada," copyright © 1964 by Mercury Press, Inc. First published in *The Magazine of Fantasy and Science Fiction*, August 1964.

"Now Is Forever," copyright © 1964 by Ziff-Davis Publishing Company. First published in *Amazing Science Fiction Stories*, March 1964.

"The Contest," copyright © 1966 by *New Worlds*.

"The Empty Room," copyright © 1966 by *New Worlds*.

"The Squirrel Cage," copyright © 1967 by *New Worlds*.

"The Number You Have Reached," copyright © 1967 by *sf Impulse*.

"1 – A," copyright © 1968 by Thomas M. Disch.

"Fun With Your New Head." An earlier version of this story, entitled "Cephalotron," originally appeared in *Playboy Magazine*, copyright © 1966 by HMH Publishing Co. Inc.

"Moondust, the Smell of Hay, and Dialectical Materialism," copyright © 1967 by Mercury Press, Inc. First published in *The Magazine of Fantasy and Science Fiction*, August 1967.

"Thesis on Social Forms and Social Controls in the U.S.A.," copyright © 1963 by Ziff-Davis Publishing Company. First published in *Fantastic*, January 1964.

"Casablanca," copyright © 1967 by Thomas M. Disch.

(The following page constitutes an extension of this copyright page.)

First published by Rupert Hart-Davis Ltd., London, 1968

This is an authorized reprint of a hardcover edition published by Doubleday & Company, Inc.

SIGNET TRADEMARK REG. U.S. PAT. OFF. AND FOREIGN COUNTRIES
REGISTERED TRADEMARK—MARCA REGISTRADA
HECHO EN CHICAGO, U.S.A.

SIGNET, SIGNET CLASSICS, SIGNETTE, MENTOR AND PLUME BOOKS
are published by The New American Library, Inc.,
1301 Avenue of the Americas, New York, New York 10019

FIRST PRINTING, FEBRUARY, 1972

PRINTED IN THE UNITED STATES OF AMERICA

To

Jerry Mundis
John Clute
Pamela Zoline
Charles and Patricia Dizenzo
patient listeners all

Contents

THE ROACHES	11
COME TO VENUS MELANCHOLY	22
LINDA AND DANIEL AND SPIKE	34
FLIGHT USELESS, INEXORABLE THE PURSUIT	41
DESCENDING	45
NADA	57
NOW IS FOREVER	77
THE CONTEST	92
THE EMPTY ROOM	96
THE SQUIRREL CAGE	99
THE NUMBER YOU HAVE REACHED	114
1–A	123
FUN WITH YOUR NEW HEAD	134
THE CITY OF PENETRATING LIGHT	137
MOONDUST, THE SMELL OF HAY, AND DIALECTICAL MATERIALISM	140
THESIS ON SOCIAL FORMS AND SOCIAL CONTROLS IN THE U.S.A.	145
CASABLANCA	158

The Roaches

Miss Marcia Kenwell had a perfect horror of cockroaches. It was an altogether different horror than the one which she felt, for instance, toward the color puce. Marcia Kenwell loathed the little things. She couldn't see one without wanting to scream. Her revulsion was so extreme that she could not bear to crush them under the soles of her shoes. No, that would be too awful. She would run, instead, for the spray can of Black Flag and inundate the little beast with poison until it ceased to move or got out of reach into one of the cracks where they all seemed to live. It was horrible, unspeakably horrible, to think of them nestling in the walls, under the linoleum, only waiting for the lights to be turned off, and then ... No, it was best not to think about it.

Every week she looked through the *Times* hoping to find another apartment, but either the rents were prohibitive (this *was* Manhattan, and Marcia's wage was a mere $62.50 a week, gross) or the building was obviously infested. She could always tell: there would be husks of dead roaches scattered about in the dust beneath the sink, stuck to the greasy backside of the stove, lining the out-of-reach cupboard shelves like the rice on the church steps after a wedding. She left such rooms in a passion of disgust, unable even to think till she reached her own apartment, where the air would be thick with the wholesome odors of Black Flag, Roach-It, and the toxic pastes that were spread on slices of potato and hidden in a hundred cracks which only she and the roaches knew about.

At least, she thought, *I keep my apartment clean.* And truly, the linoleum under the sink, the backside and underside of the stove, and the white contact paper lining her cupboards were immaculate. She could not understand

11

how other people could let these matters get so entirely out-of-hand. *They must be Puerto Ricans*, she decided—and shivered again with horror, remembering that litter of empty husks, the filth and the disease.

Such extreme antipathy toward insects—toward one particular insect—may seem excessive, but Marcia Kenwell was not really exceptional in this. There are many women, bachelor women like Marcia chiefly, who share this feeling though one may hope, for sweet charity's sake, that they escape Marcia's peculiar fate.

Marcia's phobia was, as in most such cases, hereditary in origin. That is to say, she inherited it from her mother, who had a morbid fear of anything that crawled or skittered or lived in tiny holes. Mice, frogs, snakes, worms, bugs—all could send Mrs. Kenwell into hysterics, and it would indeed have been a wonder, if little Marcia had not taken after her. It was rather strange, though, that her fear had become so particular, and stranger still that it should particularly be cockroaches that captured her fancy, for Marcia had never seen a single cockroach, didn't know what they were. (The Kenwells were a Minnesota family, and Minnesota families simply don't have cockroaches.) In fact, the subject did not arise until Marcia was nineteen and setting out (armed with nothing but a high school diploma and pluck, for she was not, you see, a very attractive girl) to conquer New York.

On the day of her departure, her favorite and only surviving aunt came with her to the Greyhound Terminal (her parents being deceased) and gave her this parting advice: "Watch out for the roaches, Marcia darling. New York City is full of cockroaches." At that time (at almost any time really) Marcia hardly paid attention to her aunt, who had opposed the trip from the start and given a hundred or more reasons why Marcia had better not go, not till she was older at least.

Her aunt had been proven right on all counts: Marcia after five years and fifteen employment agency fees could find nothing in New York but dull jobs at mediocre wages; she had no more friends than when she lived on West 16th; and, except for its view (the Chock Full O'Nuts warehouse and a patch of sky), her present apartment on lower Thompson Street was not a great improvement on its predecessor.

The city was full of promises, but they had all been

The Roaches

pledged to other people. The city Marcia knew was sinful, indifferent, dirty, and dangerous. Every day she read accounts of women attacked in subway stations, raped in the streets, knifed in their own beds. A hundred people looked on curiously all the while and offered no assistance. And on top of everything else there were the roaches!

There were roaches everywhere, but Marcia didn't see them until she'd been in New York a month. They came to her—or she to them—at Silversmith's on Nassau Street, a stationery shop where she had been working for three days. It was the first job she'd been able to find. Alone or helped by a pimply stockboy (in all fairness it must be noted that Marcia was not without an acne problem of her own), she wandered down rows of rasp-edged metal shelves in the musty basement, making an inventory of the sheaves and piles and boxes of bond paper, leatherette-bound diaries, pins and clips, and carbon paper. The basement was dirty and so dim that she needed a flashlight for the lowest shelves. In the obscurest corner, a faucet leaked perpetually into a gray sink: she had been resting near this sink, sipping a cup of tepid coffee (saturated, in the New York manner, with sugar and drowned in milk), thinking, probably, of how she could afford several things she simply couldn't afford, when she noticed the dark spots moving on the side of the sink. At first she thought they might be no more than motes floating in the jelly of her eyes, or the giddy dots that one sees after over-exertion on a hot day. But they persisted too long to be illusory, and Marcia drew nearer, feeling compelled to bear witness. *How do I know they are insects?* she thought.

How are we to explain the fact that what repels us most can be at times—at the same time—inordinately attractive? Why is the cobra poised to strike so beautiful? The fascination of the abomination is something that . . . Something which we would rather not account for. The subject borders on the obscene, and there is no need to deal with it here, except to note the breathless wonder with which Marcia observed these first roaches of hers. Her chair was drawn so close to the sink that she could see the mottling of their oval, unsegmented bodies, the quick scuttering of their thin legs, and the quicker flutter of their antennae. They moved randomly, proceeding nowhere, centered nowhere. They seemed greatly disturbed over nothing. *Perhaps,* Marcia thought, *my presence has a morbid effect on them?*

Only then did she become aware, aware fully, that these were the cockroaches of which she had been warned. Repulsion took hold; her flesh curdled on her bones. She screamed and fell back in her chair, almost upsetting a shelf of odd-lots. Simultaneously the roaches disappeared over the edge of the sink and into the drain.

Mr. Silversmith, coming downstairs to inquire the source of Marcia's alarm, found her supine and unconscious. He sprinkled her face with tapwater, and she awoke with a shudder of nausea. She refused to explain why she had screamed and insisted that she must leave Mr. Silversmith's employ immediately. He, supposing that the pimply stockboy (who was his son) had made a pass at Marcia, paid her for the three days she had worked and let her go without regrets. From that moment on, cockroaches were to be a regular feature of Marcia's existence.

On Thompson Street Marcia was able to reach a sort of stalemate with the cockroaches. She settled into a comfortable routine of pastes and powders, scrubbing and waxing, prevention (she never had even a cup of coffee without washing and drying cup and coffeepot immediately afterward) and ruthless extermination. The only roaches who trespassed upon her two cozy rooms came up from the apartment below, and they did not stay long, you may be sure. Marcia would have complained to the landlady, except that it was the landlady's apartment and her roaches. She had been inside, for a glass of wine on Christmas Eve, and she had to admit that it wasn't exceptionally dirty. It was, in fact, more than commonly clean—but *that* was not enough in New York. *If everyone,* Marcia thought, *took as much care as I, there would soon be no cockroaches in New York City.*

Then (it was March and Marcia was halfway through her sixth year in the city) the Shchapalovs moved in next door. There were three of them—two men and a woman—and they were old, though exactly how old it was hard to say: they had been aged by more than time. Perhaps they weren't more than forty. The woman, for instance, though she still had brown hair, had a face wrinkly as a prune and was missing several teeth. She would stop Marcia in the hallway or on the street, grabbing hold of her coatsleeve, and talk to her—always a simple lament about the weather, which was too hot or too cold or too wet or too dry. Marcia never knew half of what the old woman was saying, she mumbled so. Then she'd totter off to the grocery with her bagful of empties.

The Shchapalovs, you see, drank. Marcia, who had a rather exaggerated idea of the cost of alcohol (the cheapest thing she could imagine was vodka), wondered where they got the money for all the drinking they did. She knew they didn't work, for on days when Marcia was home with the flu she could hear the three Shchapalovs through the thin wall between their kitchen and hers screaming at each other to exercise their adrenal glands. *They're on welfare,* Marcia decided. Or perhaps the man with only one eye was a veteran on pension.

She didn't so much mind the noise of their arguments (she was seldom home in the afternoon), but she couldn't stand their singing. Early in the evening they'd start in, singing along with the radio stations. Everything they listened to sounded like Guy Lombardo. Later, about eight o'clock they sang *a cappella*. Strange, soulless noises rose and fell like Civil Defense sirens; there were bellowings, bayings, and cries. Marcia had heard something like it once on a Folkways record of Czechoslovakian wedding chants. She was quite beside herself whenever the awful noise started up and had to leave the house till they were done. A complaint would do no good: the Shchapalovs had a right to sing at that hour.

Besides, one of the men was said to be related by marriage to the landlady. That's how they got the apartment, which had been used as a storage space until they'd moved in. Marcia couldn't understand how the three of them could fit into such a little space—just a room-and-a-half with a narrow window opening onto the air shaft. (Marcia had discovered that she could see their entire living space through a hole that had been broken through the wall when the plumbers had installed a sink for the Shchapalovs.)

But if their singing distressed her, *what* was she to do about the roaches? The Shchapalov woman, who was the sister of one man and married to the other—or else the men were brothers and she was the wife of one of them (sometimes, it seemed to Marcia, from the words that came through the walls, that she was married to neither of them—or to both), was a bad housekeeper, and the Shchapalov apartment was soon swarming with roaches. Since Marcia's sink and the Shchapalovs' were fed by the same pipes and emptied into a common drain, a steady overflow of roaches was disgorged into Marcia's immaculate kitchen. She could spray and lay out more poisoned potatoes; she could scrub and dust and stuff Kleenex tissues into holes where the pipes passed through the wall: it was all to no avail. The Shchapalov roaches could always lay another million eggs in the garbage bags rotting beneath the Shchapalov sink. In a few days they would be swarming through the pipes and cracks and into Marcia's cupboards. She would lay in bed and watch them (this was possible because Marcia kept a nightlight burning in each room) advancing across the floor and up the walls, trailing the Shchapalovs' filth and disease everywhere they went.

One such evening the roaches were especially bad, and Marcia was trying to muster the resolution to get out of her warm bed and attack them with Roach-It. She had left the windows open from the conviction that cockroaches do not like the cold, but she found that she liked it much less. When she swallowed, it hurt, and she knew she was coming down with a cold. And all because of *them!*

"*Oh go away!*" she begged. "*Go away! Go away! Get out of my apartment.*"

She addressed the roaches with the same desperate intensity with which she sometimes (though not often in recent years) addressed prayers to the Almighty. Once she had prayed all night long to get rid of her acne, but in the morning it was worse than ever. People in intolerable circumstances will pray to anything. Truly, there are no atheists in foxholes: the men there pray to the bombs that they may land somewhere else.

The only strange thing in Marcia's case is that her prayers were answered. The cockroaches fled from her apartment as quickly as their little legs could carry them— and in straight lines, too. Had they heard her? Had they understood?

Marcia could still see one cockroach coming down from the cupboard. "*Stop!*" she commanded. And it stopped.

At Marcia's spoken command, the cockroach would

march up and down, to the left and to the right. Suspecting that her phobia had matured into madness, Marcia left her warm bed, turned on the light, and cautiously approached the roach, which remained motionless, as she had bidden it. *"Wiggle your antennas,"* she commanded. The cockroach wiggled its antennae.

She wondered if they would *all* obey her and found, within the next few days, that they all would. They would do anything she told them to. They would eat poison out of her hand. Well, not exactly out of her hand, but it amounted to the same thing. They were devoted to her. Slavishly.

It is the end, she thought, *of my roach problem.* But of course it was only the beginning.

Marcia did not question too closely the *reason* the roaches obeyed her. She had never much troubled herself with abstract problems. After expending so much time and attention on them, it seemed only natural that she should exercise a certain power over them. However she was wise enough never to speak of this power to anyone else—even to Miss Bismuth at the insurance office. Miss Bismuth read the horoscope magazines and claimed to be able to communicate with her mother, aged sixty-eight, telepathically. Her mother lived in Ohio. But what would Marcia have said: that *she* could communicate telepathically with cockroaches? Impossible.

Nor did Marcia use her power for any other purpose than keeping the cockroaches out of her own apartment. Whenever she saw one, she simply commanded it to go to the Shchapalov apartment and stay there. It was surprising then that there were always more roaches coming back through the pipes. Marcia assumed that they were younger generations. Cockroaches are known to breed fast. But it was easy enough to send them back to the Shchapalovs.

"Into their beds," she added as an afterthought. *"Go into their beds."* Disgusting as it was, the idea gave her a queer thrill of pleasure.

The next morning, the Shchapalov woman, smelling a little worse than usual (Whatever was it, Marcia wondered, that they drank?), was waiting at the open door of her apartment. She wanted to speak to Marcia before she left for work. Her housedress was mired from an attempt at scrubbing the floor, and while she sat there talking, she tried to wring out the scrubwater.

"No idea!" she exclaimed. "You ain't got no idea how bad! 'S terrible!"

"What?" Marcia asked, knowing perfectly well what.

"The boogs! Oh, the boogs are just everywhere. Don't you have em, sweetheart? I don't know what to do. I try to keep a decent house, God knows—" She lifted her rheumy eyes to heaven, testifying. "—but I don't know what to do." She leaned forward, confidingly. "You won't believe this, sweetheart, but last night . . ." A cockroach began to climb out of the limp strands of hair straggling down into the woman's eyes. ". . . they got into bed with us! Would you believe it? There must have been a hundred of 'em. I said to Osip, I said—What's wrong, sweetheart?"

Marcia, speechless with horror, pointed at the roach, which had almost reached the bridge of the woman's nose. "Yech!" the woman agreed, smashing it and wiping her dirtied thumb on her dirtied dress. "Goddam boogs! I hate em, I swear to God. But what's a person gonna do? Now, what I wanted to ask, sweetheart, is do you have a problem with the boogs? Being as how you're right next door, I thought—" She smiled a confidential smile, as though to say this is just between us ladies. Marcia almost expected a roach to skitter out between her gapped teeth.

"No," she said. "No, I use Black Flag." She backed away from the doorway toward the safety of the stairwell. "Black Flag," she said again, louder. "Black Flag," she shouted from the foot of the stairs. Her knees trembled so, that she had to hold onto the metal banister for support.

At the insurance office that day, Marcia couldn't keep her mind on her work five minutes at a time. (Her work in the Actuarial Dividends department consisted of adding up long rows of two-digit numbers on a Burroughs adding machine and checking the similar additions of her co-workers for errors.) She kept thinking of the cockroaches in the tangled hair of the Shchapalov woman, of her bed teeming with roaches, and of other, less concrete horrors on the periphery of consciousness. The numbers swam and swarmed before her eyes, and twice she had to go to the Ladies' Room, but each time it was a false alarm. Nevertheless, lunchtime found her with no appetite. Instead of going down to the employee cafeteria she went out into the fresh April air and strolled along 23rd Street. Despite the spring, it all seemed to bespeak a sordidness, a festering corruption. The stones of the Flatiron Building oozed damp blackness; the gutters were heaped with soft decay; the smell of burning grease hung in the air outside the cheap restaurants like cigarette smoke in a close room.

The afternoon was worse. Her fingers would not touch the correct numbers on the machine unless she looked at them. One silly phrase kept running through her head: "Something must be done. Something must be done." She had quite forgotten that she had sent the roaches into the Shchapalovs' bed in the first place.

That night, instead of going home immediately, she went to a double feature on 42nd Street. She couldn't afford the better movies. Susan Hayward's little boy almost drowned in quicksand. That was the only thing she remembered afterward.

She did something that she had never done before. She had a drink in a bar. She had two drinks. Nobody bothered her; nobody even looked in her direction. She took a taxi to Thompson Street (the subways weren't safe at that hour) and arrived at her door by eleven o'clock. She didn't have anything left for a tip. The taxi driver said he understood.

There was a light on under the Shchapalovs' door, and they were singing. It was eleven o'clock. "Something must be done," Marcia whispered to herself earnestly. "Something must be *done*."

Without turning on her own light, without even taking off her new spring jacket from Ohrbach's, Marcia got down on her knees and crawled under the sink. She tore out the Kleenexes she had stuffed into the cracks around the pipes.

There they were, the three of them, the Shchapalovs, drinking, the woman plumped on the lap of the one-eyed man, and the other man, in a dirty undershirt, stamping his foot on the floor to accompany the loud discords of their song. Horrible. They were drinking of course, she might have known it, and now the woman pressed her roachy mouth against the mouth of the one-eyed man— kiss, kiss. Horrible, horrible. Marcia's hands knotted into her mouse-colored hair, and she thought: *The filth, the disease!* Why, they hadn't learned a thing from last night!

Some time later (Marcia had lost track of time) the overhead light in the Shchapalovs' apartment was turned off. Marcia waited till they made no more noise. "Now," Marcia said, "all of you.

"All of you in this building, all of you that can hear me, gather round the bed, but wait a little while yet. Patience. All of you . . ." The words of her command fell apart into little fragments, which she told like the beads of a rosary—little brown ovoid wooden beads. ". . . gather round . . . wait a little while yet . . . all of you . . . patience . . . gather round . . ." Her hand stroked the cold water pipes rhythmically, and it seemed that she could hear them—gathering, scuttering up through the walls, coming out of the cupboards, the garbage bags—a host, an army, and she was their absolute queen.

"Now!" she said. "Mount them! Cover them! Devour them!"

There was no doubt that she could hear them now. She heard them quite palpably. Their sound was like grass in the wind, like the first stirrings of gravel dumped from a truck. Then there was the Shchapalov woman's scream, and curses from the men, such terrible curses that Marcia could hardly bear to listen.

A light went on, and Marcia could see them, the roaches, everywhere. Every surface, the walls, the floors, the shabby sticks of furniture, was mottly thick with *Blattelae Germanicae*. There was more than a single thickness.

The Shchapalov woman, standing up in her bed, screamed monotonously. Her pink rayon nightgown was speckled with brown-black dots. Her knobby fingers tried to brush bugs out of her hair, off her face. The man in the undershirt who a few minutes before had been stomping his feet to the music stomped now more urgently, one hand still holding onto the lightcord. Soon the floor was slimy with crushed roaches, and he slipped. The light went out. The woman's scream took on a rather choked quality, as though . . .

But Marcia wouldn't think of that. "Enough," she whispered. "No more. Stop."

She crawled away from the sink, across the room on to her bed, which tried, with a few tawdry cushions, to dissemble itself as a couch for the daytime. Her breathing came hard, and there was a curious constriction in her throat. She was sweating incontinently.

From the Shchapalovs' room came scuffling sounds, a door banged, running feet, and then a louder, muffled noise, perhaps a body falling downstairs. The landlady's voice: "What the hell do you think you're—" Other voices overriding hers. Incoherences, and footsteps returning up the stairs. Once more, the landlady: "There ain't no *boogs* here, for heaven's sake. The boogs is in your heads. You've got the d.t.'s, that's what. And it wouldn't be any wonder, if there were boogs. The place is filthy. Look at that crap on the floor. Filth! I've stood just about enough from you. Tomorrow you move out, hear? This *used* to be a decent building."

The Shchapalovs did not protest their eviction. Indeed, they did not wait for the morrow to leave. They quitted their apartment with only a suitcase, a laundry bag, and an electric toaster. Marcia watched them go down the steps through her half-open door. *It's done,* she thought. *It's all over.*

With a sigh of almost sensual pleasure, she turned on the lamp beside the bed, then the other lamps. The room gleamed immaculately. Deciding to celebrate her victory, she went to the cupboard, where she kept a bottle of *crème de menthe.*

The cupboard was full of roaches.

She had not told them where to go, where *not* to go, when they left the Shchapalov apartment. It was her own fault.

The great silent mass of roaches regarded Marcia calmly, and it seemed to the distracted girl that she could read *their* thoughts, their thought rather, for they had but a single thought. She could read it as clearly as she could read the illuminated billboard for Chock Full O'Nuts outside her window. It was delicate as music issuing from a thousand tiny pipes. It was an ancient music box open after centuries of silence: "We love you we love you we love you we love you."

Something strange happened inside Marcia then, something unprecedented: she responded.

"I love you too," she replied. "Oh, I love you. Come to me, all of you. Come to me. I love you. Come to me. I love you. Come to me."

From every corner of Manhattan, from the crumbling walls of Harlem, from restaurants on 56th Street, from warehouses along the river, from sewers and from orange peels moldering in garbage cans, the loving roaches came forth and began to crawl toward their mistress.

Come to Venus Melancholy

Is that you, John? Did someone just come in the door? Of course, it wouldn't be John. Not after all this time. It was because I was startled I said that. If you're there, whoever you are, do you mind if I talk to you?

And if you're not there?

Then I suppose you'll mind even less.

Maybe it was just the wind. Can the wind lift a latch? Maybe the latch is broken. Though it feels all right now. Or maybe I'm hallucinating. That's what happened, you know, in the classic sense-deprivation experiments. But I guess my case is different. I guess they've rigged me up some way so that can't happen.

Or maybe—Christ, I hope not! Maybe one of those hairy caterpillar things has got inside. I really couldn't stand that—thinking of the whole house, thinking of *me*, crawling with those things. I've always hated bugs. So if you don't mind, I'll close the door.

Have you been trying to talk to me? I should have told you it's no use. I can't hear and I can't see. I'm broken. Do you see, there in the larger room, in each corner, about five feet from the floor, how they've been smashed? My eyes and ears. Can't they be fixed somehow? If it's only a matter of vacuum tubes and diaphragms, there should be things of that sort downstairs. I'm opening the trapdoor now—do you see? And I've turned the lights on in the storeroom.

Oh hell, what's the use?

I mean *you're* probably not there, and even if you are, *he* probably thought to smash any spare tubes that were left. He thought of everything else.

Ah, but he was so handsome, he was really so handsome. He wasn't tall. After all, the ceiling here isn't much over six feet. But he was well-proportioned. He had deep-set eyes and a low brow. Sometimes, when he was worried or puzzled, he looked positively neanderthal.

John George Clay, that was his name. It sounds like part of a poem, doesn't it? John George Clay.

It wasn't so much his features—it was his manner. He took himself so seriously. And he was so dumb. It was that combination—the earnestness and the stupidity—that got to me. A sort of maternity syndrome I guess you'd call it. After all, I couldn't very well be his wife, could I? Oh, when I think . . .

Excuse me, I must be boring you. I'm sure you can't be that interested in a machine's love life. Perhaps I could read something aloud? He wasn't able to get at the microfilm library, so there's still plenty of books. When I'm by myself I don't do anything but read. It gets to seem as though the whole world was made of print. I look at it not for what's written there but as though it were a landscape. But I digress.

What do you like; poetry? novels? science texbooks? the encyclopedia? I've read all of it so many times I could puke, if you'll excuse the expression. Whoever selected those books never heard of the twentieth century. There's nothing later than Robert Browning and Thomas Hardy— and would you believe it?—some of *that* has been expurgated? What did they think? That Browning would corrupt my morals? Or John's? Who can understand the bureaucratic mind?

Personally, I prefer poetry. You don't get tired of it so quickly. But maybe there's something you need to know, a point of information? If you could only *talk* to me. There must be some way to fix one of the mikes, there has to. Oh, *please!*

Oh hell.

I'm sorry, but it's just that it's so hard to believe that you're there. It gets to seem that I only talk to hear myself speak. I wish to God I *could* hear myself speak.

Maybe I just sound like static to you. Maybe he smashed the speakers too, I wouldn't be surprised. I don't know. There's no way I can tell. But I try my best, I think each word very slowly and try to enunciate mentally. And that way the caterpillars won't be confused. Ha!

I'm really glad you've come. I've been so long without company that I'm grateful even for the illusion of it. Don't take offense: since I can't ever be sure that you're there, you can't be more than illusion for me, whether you're real or not. A paradox. I welcome you in either case. With my doors wide open.

It's been fifteen years. Fifteen years, four months, twelve days—and three hours. I've got this built-in clock connected to what used to be the nerves of my stomach. I'm never in doubt about the time. It's always right there—like a bellyache. There've been whole days when I just listen to myself tick.

I was human once, you know. A married woman, with two children and a Master's in English Lit. A lot of good that ever did. My thesis was on some letters Milton wrote when he was Cromwell's Latin Secretary. Dull? You'd better believe it. Only I'll ever know *how* dull.

And yet ... now ... I'd give this whole damn planet to be back there in the academic squirrel cage, spinning that beautiful, dull wheel.

Do you like Milton? I've got the Complete Works, except for the things he wrote in Latin. I could read you something, if you'd like.

I used to read things to John, but he didn't much appreciate it. He enjoyed mysteries now and then. Or he'd study an electronics text under the scanner. But poetry bored him. It was worse than that: he seemed to hate poetry.

But maybe you're not like that. How can I tell? Do you mind if I just read it aloud for my own sake? Poetry's meant to be read aloud.

Il Penseroso. Do you know it? It gives me goosebumps every time. Figuratively.

Are you listening, caterpillars?

How did you like that?

> *These pleasures, Melancholy, give,*
> *And I with thee will choose to live.*

Well, it's all a lot of gas. That's what dear John called it. He called it other things too, and in each case I've come at last to agree. But such lovely gas. John couldn't see that. He was a very simple sort, was John, and blind to the beauty of almost anything except a rip-snorting sunset. And nude women. He was uncomplicated. Without a sense of dialectics. He probably didn't understand half the things I said to him. If ever there was a mismatched couple, it was us.

Spacemen and pioneers, you know, are supposed to be brighter than average. And maybe John's IQ was a bit over one hundred but not by much, not by half a sigma distance. After all, what did he need intelligence for? He was only a glorified fur-trader. He'd go out into the swamp and hunt around for the slugs the caterpillars laid there. He'd find one, maybe two, a day and keep them undernourished so they'd grow slower. Every three weeks the ship would come along, pick up the slugs, and leave supplies.

I don't know what the slugs were for. They secreted something hallucinogenic, but whether they were using it to cure psychoses or produce them, I never found out. There was a war going on then, and my theory was that it all had something to do with bacteriological warfare.

Maybe the war is still going on. But my theory—my *other* theory, I have lots of them—is that the war is over and both sides have killed each other off. Otherwise, wouldn't someone have come here for me by now?

But maybe they have—maybe that's why *you're* here! Is it?

Or maybe they don't care. Maybe I'm considered expendable.

Maybe, maybe, maybe! Oh God I could scream!

There now, I'm better again. These things pass.

Let me introduce myself. I've lost my good manners living out here alone like this. My name is Selma Meret Hoffer. Hoffer's my maiden name. I use it now that I'm divorced.

Why don't I tell you my story? It will pass the time as well as anything. There's nothing much to tell about the time I was human. I won't say I was ordinary—nobody ever believes that of themselves—but I probably didn't stand out in a crowd. In fact, I tried very hard not to. I'm the introvert type.

I was only thirty-two when I found out I had leukemia. The clinic gave me six months. The alternative was this. Of course I chose this. I thought I was lucky I could qualify. Most people don't have an alternative. Of those who do, few refuse. In a way it seemed like an afterlife. The operation was certainly a good facsimile of death.

After surgery they used fancy acids that attacked the body tissues selectively. Anaesthetics didn't help much then. They whittled me down to the bare nerves and dumped me into this tank and sealed me in.

Voila—the Cyborg!

Between the sealing-in and the shipping off there were months and months while I was being wired up with the auxiliary memory banks and being taught to use my motor nerves again. It's quite a traumatic experience, losing your body, and the tendency is to go catatonic. What else is there to *do* after all? Naturally I don't remember much of that time.

They brought me out of it with shock treatment, and the first thing I remember was this room. It was stark and antiseptic then. I suppose it still is, but then it was starker and more antiseptic. I hated it with a passion. The walls were that insipid creamy-green that's supposed to prevent eyestrain. They must have got the furniture from a fire sale at the Bauhaus. It was all aluminum tubes and swatches of bright-colored canvas. And even so, by some miracle of design the room managed to seem cramped. It's fifteen feet square, but then it seemed no bigger than a coffin. I wanted to run right out of that room—and then I realized I couldn't: I was the room, the room was me.

I learned to talk very quickly so I could give them directions for redecorating. They argued at first. "But, Miss Hoffer," they'd say, "we can't take an ounce more payload, and this furniture is Regulation." That was the name of their god, Regulation. I said if it took an act of Congress they'd redecorate, and at last I got my way. Looking back on it, I suspect the whole thing was done to keep me busy. Those first few months when you're learning to think of yourself as a machine can be pretty rife with horror. A lot of the cyborgs just go psycho—usually it's some compulsion mechanism. They just keep repeating the Star-Spangled Banner or say the rosary or some such thing. Like a machine.

They say it's not the same thing—a cybernetic organism and a machine, but what do they know about it? They're not cyborgs.

Even when I was human I was never any good at mechanical things. I could never remember which way you turned a screwdriver to put in a screw—and there I was with my motor nerves controlling a whole miniature factory of whatsits and thingumbobs. My index finger powered a Mixmaster. My middle toe turned the tumblers that locked the door. My . . .

That reminds me: have I locked you in? I'm sorry, when I closed the door I locked it without thinking. You wouldn't want to go out now though. According to my stomach, it's the middle of the night. You're better off in here for the night than in a Venusian swamp, eh?

Well, that's the story of my life. When I had the reflexes of a well-trained rat, they packed me up and shipped me off to Venus at the cost of some few million dollars.

The very last thing I learned before leaping was how to use the microfilm scanner. I read direct from the spindle. By the time I learned how poorly the library had been stocked it was too late to complain. I'd been planted out in the swamp, and John George Clay had moved in. What did I care about the library then? I was in love.

And what do *you* care about any of this? Unless you're a cyberneticist doing a study on malfunction. I should be good for a chapter, at least.

Excuse me, I'm probably keeping you awake. I'll let you get some sleep. I have to sleep sometimes myself, you know. Physically I can go without, but I still have a subconscious that likes to dream—

> *Of forests and enchantments drear,*
> *Where more is meant than meets the ear.*

And so good night.

Still awake?

I couldn't go to sleep myself, so I've been reading. I thought maybe you'd like to hear a poem. I'll read you *Il Penseroso*. Do you know it? It's probably the finest poem in the language. It's by John Milton.

Oh dear, did I keep you up with that poem last night? Or did I only dream that I did? If I was noisy, you'll excuse me, won't you?

Now if you were John, you'd be raging mad. He didn't like to be woken up by—

> *Such notes as, warbled to the string,*
> *Drew iron tears down Pluto's cheek*
> *And made Hell grant what Love did seek!*

Indeed he didn't. John had a strange and fixed distaste for that wonderful poem, which is probably the finest in the language. He was, I think, jealous of it. It was a part of me he could never possess, even though I was his slave in so many other ways. Or is "housekeeper" a more polite expression?

I tried to explain the more difficult parts to him, the mythology and the exotic words, but he didn't *want* to understand. He made fun of it. He had a way of saying the lines that made them seem ridiculous. Mincingly, like this:

> *Come, pensive Nun, devout and pure,*
> *Sober, steadfast, and demure.*

When he'd do that, I'd just ignore him. I'd recite it to myself. He'd usually leave the house then, even if it was night. He knew I worried myself sick when he was away. He did it deliberately. He had a genius for cruelty.

I suppose you're wondering if it worked both ways—whether he loved me. The question must have occurred to you. I've given it quite a lot of thought myself, and I've come to the conclusion that he did. The trouble was he didn't know how to express it. Our relationship was necessarily so *cerebral*, and cerebration wasn't John's *forte*.

That was the idea behind throwing us together the way they did. They couldn't very well send a man off by himself for two years. He'd go crazy. Previously they'd sent married couples, but the homicide rate was incredible. Something like 30 per cent. It's one thing for a pioneer family to be off by itself in, say, the Yukon. It's something else here. In a social vacuum like this, sex is explosive.

You see, apart from going out for the slugs and nursing them in the shed outside, there's nothing to do. You can't build out here. Things just sort of sink into the mud unless, like me, they're built like a houseboat. You can't grow things—including children. It's a biologist's paradise, but they need hundreds of slug stations and there aren't biologists available in that quantity. Besides, all the *good*

Come to Venus Melancholy

biologists are in Venusburg, where there's research facilities. The problem then is to find the minimum number of personnel that can man a station for two years of idleness without exploding. The solution is one man and one cyborg.

Though not, as you can see, an infallible solution. I tried to kill him, you know. It was a silly thing to do. I regret it now.

But I'd rather not talk about it, if you don't mind.

You've been here two days now—fancy that!

Excuse me for keeping to myself so long, but I had a sudden, acute attack of self-consciousness, and the only cure for that is solitude. I invoke Milton's lovely Melancholy, and then everything is better. The beasts quiet down. Eurydice is set free again. Hell freezes over. Ha!

But that's a lot of nonsense. Let's not talk always about me. Let's talk about *you*. Who are you? What are you like? How long will you be staying here on Venus? Two days we've been together and still I know nothing about you.

Shall I tell you what I imagine you to be like? You're tall—though I hope not so tall as to find that low room uncomfortable—with laughing blue eyes and a deep spaceman's tan. You're strong yet gentle, gay yet basically serious. You're getting rather hungry.

And everywhere you go you leave little green slugs behind you that look like runny lime Jell-O.

Oh hell, excuse me. I'm always saying excuse me. I'm sick of it. I'm sick of half-truths and reticences.

Does that frighten you? Do you want out already? Don't go now—I've just *begun* to fight. Listen to the whole story, and then—maybe—I'll unlock the door.

By the way, in case you are getting hungry there may still be some rations left down in the storeroom. I don't want it to be said that I'm lacking in hospitality. I'll open the trapdoor and turn on the light, but you'll have to look for them yourself. Of course, you're worried that I'll lock you in down there. Well, I can't promise that I won't. After all, how do I know you're *not* John? Can you prove it? You can't even prove you exist!

I'll leave the trapdoor open in case you should change your mind.

For my next number I'd like to do *Il Penseroso* by

John Milton. Quiet down, caterpillars, and listen. It's the finest poem in the language.

How about that? Makes you want to go right out and join a Trappist monastery, doesn't it? That's what John once said.

I'll say one thing for John: he never tattled. He could have had me taken away and turned to scrap. All he had to do was give the word when the ship came down to pick up the slugs, but when there was company he could always put a good face on things. He was a gentleman in every sense of the word.

How did it happen then—if he was a gentleman and I was a lady? Whose fault was it? Good God, I've asked myself that question a hundred times. It was both our faults and neither's. It was the fault of the situation.

I can't remember now which of us was the first to start talking about sex. We talked about everything that first year, and sex is very much a part of everything. What harm could there be in it, after all, with me sealed in a steel tank? And how could we *avoid* the subject? He'd mention an old girlfriend or tell a slightly shady joke, and I'd be reminded of something by degrees . . .

The thing is that there's an immense curiosity between the sexes that almost never is satisfied. Things that men never know about women, and vice versa. Even between a man and a wife, there is a gulf of unmentionables. Maybe especially between a man and a wife. But between John and me there seemed to be nothing to prevent perfect candor. What possible harm could it do?

Then . . . the next thing . . . I don't remember which of us started that either. We should have known better. The borderline between perfect candor and erotic fantasy is no wider than an adjective. But it happened inperceptibly, and before we knew quite what we were doing, it had been done. It was already a habit.

When I realized exactly what we were doing, of course, I laid down the law. It was an unhealthy situation, it had to stop. At first John was agreeable. He was embarrassed, like a little boy who's been found out in some naughtiness. We told each other it was over and done with.

But it had become, as I've said, a habit. I have a rather more vivid imagination than John and he had grown dependent on me. He asked for new stories, and I refused.

He got angry then and wouldn't speak to me, and finally I gave in. I was in love with him, you see, in my own ectoplasmic way, and this was all I could do to show it.

Every day he wanted a new story. It's hard to make the same tired old tale seem new in every telling. Scheherazade was supposed to have stood up for a thousand and one nights, but after only thirty I was wearing thin. Under the strain I sort of retreated into myself.

I read poetry, lots of poetry, but mostly Milton. Milton has a very calming effect on me—like a mil-town if you'll excuse the pun.

The pun—that's what did it. It was the last turn of the screw, a simple pun.

It seems that when I read, I sometimes read aloud without realizing it. That's what John has told me. It was all right during the day when he was off in the swamp, and when he was here in the evenings we'd talk with each other. But he needed more sleep than I did, and when I was left on my own, after he'd gone to bed, I'd read. There was nothing else to do. Usually I'd read some long Victorian novel, but at the time I'm speaking of, I mostly read *Il Penseroso*.

He *shouldn't* have made fun of it. I guess he didn't realize how important it had become to me. It was like a pool of pure water in which I could wash away the grime of each day. Or else he was angry for being woken up.

Do you remember the part, right near the beginning, where it says:

> "But hail, thou goddess sage and holy,
> Hail divinest Melancholy"?

Of course you do. You probably know the whole thing as well as I do by now. Well, when John heard that he broke out laughing, a nasty laugh, and I, well, I couldn't really stand that, could I? I mean Milton means so *much* to me, and the thing was that he began to sing this *song*. This awful song. Oh, it was a clever idea, I suppose, when first he thought of it, but the combination of that vulgar tune and his perversion of Milton's noble words—though he claims that's how he understood the words when I first read them to him, and I still maintain that the second *i* in divinest is pronounced like a long *e*—it was aggravating in the extreme, I can't tell you how much it upset me.

Do I *have* to repeat them?

> *Come to Venus, Melancholy Baby.*
> *Cuddle up and don't by shy.*

And so on. It's not only a bad pun—it's a misquotation as well. It should be *Hail*, not *Come*. So vulgar. It gives me goosebumps even now.

I told him to leave the house right that minute. I told him not to come back till he was ready to apologize. I was so angry I forgot it was the middle of the night. As soon as he was out the door, I was ashamed of myself.

He came back in five minutes. He apologized outside the door, and I let him in. He had the large polyethylene bag over his shoulder that he uses to gather up the slugs, but I was so relieved I didn't think anything of it.

He put them on the visual receptors. There must have been twenty, all told, and each one was about a foot long. They fought each other to get right on the lens because it was slightly warmer there. There were twenty of them, foul, gelatinous slugs, crawling on my *eyes*, oh God, I shut my eyes and I shut off my ears, because he was singing that song again, and I locked the doors and I left him like that for five days while I recited *Il Penseroso*.

But whenever I came to that one line, I could never say it.

It was perhaps the hallucinogens, though he might just as well have done it in his right mind. He had every reason to. But I prefer to think it was the hallucinogens. He had been all that time with nothing else to eat. I've never been five days without food, so I don't know how desperate that would make one.

In any case, when I came to myself again and opened my eyes I found I had no eyes to open. He'd smashed every receptor in the room, even the little mobile attachment for cleaning. The strange thing was how little I cared. It seemed hardly to matter at all.

I opened the door for five minutes so he could get out. Then I closed it so no more caterpillars could get in. But unlocked. That way John was free to come back.

But he never did.

The supply ship was due in two days later, and I guess John must have spent that time in the shed where he kept the slugs. He must have been alive, otherwise the pilot of the supply ship would have come in the door to look for him. And nobody ever came in the door again.

Unless you did.

They just left me here, deaf and blind and half-immortal, in the middle of the Venusian swamp. If only I could starve to death—or wear out—or rust—or really go insane. But I'm too well made for that. You'd think after all the money they spent on me, they'd want to salvage what they could, wouldn't you?

I have a deal to make with you. I'll let you out the door, if you'll do something for me. Fair enough?

Down in the storeroom there are explosives. They're so safe a child could use them. John did, after all. If I remember rightly, they're on the third shelf down on the west wall—little black boxes with DANGER written on them in red. You pull out the little pin and set the timing menhanism for anything from five minutes to an hour. It's just like an alarm clock.

Once they're set, just leave them in the storeroom. They'll be nearer to me down there. I'm over the storeroom. Then run like hell. Five minutes should be time enough, shouldn't it? I'll only want to read a bit of *Il Penseroso*.

Is it a deal? The trapdoor is open, and I'm opening the outside door now just to show you I'm in earnest.

While you set to work, I think I'll read something to pass the time.

Hello? I'm waiting. Is everything all right? Are you still there? Or were you ever there? Oh please, *please*—I want to explode. That would be so wonderful. Please, I *beg* of you!

I'm still waiting.

Linda and Daniel and Spike

"Most men are too, you know, unintelligent," Linda explained to her imaginary friend Daniel, while they were walking through Central Park. She was not what you would have called an attractive girl. Her nose was decidedly too large, and she had an unpleasant way, when speaking, of giving strident and undue emphasis to particular words.

It was night, a cool summer night, and Linda had allowed Daniel to hold her hand.

"They're only interested in one thing, if you know what I mean. Whereas *you*, you're different somehow. When we talk like this together, I seem to understand things that I didn't understand before. It's like ... oh, I don't know how to say it. Do you know what I mean?"

Daniel nodded.

"It's like you were my father and I were just a little girl. Or it's like you were a priest listening to my confession. You *know* so many different things, things I'd never heard of till I met you: Science! The theater! Politics! Psychology! Interesting things like that. I should have gone on to college. I guess that was where I made my mistake. Essentially I'm what you call the intellectual type. But you know how kids are—impatient. So I didn't go. I suppose you must think I'm awful dumb?"

"Oh no!" said Daniel. He seemed shocked.

"But you must have thought so when you first met me. Jesus, I was dumb then. I didn't know *anything*. Did I? Nothing. Not a *thing*. I mean, I didn't know about S-E-X."

She giggled when Daniel squeezed her hand with unmistakable meaning. "Now don't you start that again!" she scolded.

"No?"

"You old Casanova! Do you know what? The very first time I ever set eyes on you, at Roseland last year, I said to myself then, 'Now there is a man to watch out for.' I was just sitting there, you know, watching the people dance, and I saw you. I said, 'There is a *dang*-erous man.' I've never seen *anyone* who could waltz like you can. I suppose some people would say that's old hat, waltzing."

"Oh?"

She smiled generously. "But not me! I think the waltz is just about the most beautiful dance in the world, to say the very least. And I think that you . . . that I . . ."

Without warning she broke into tears. Daniel helped her to a park bench, for she seemed to have grown unsteady on her feet. He kissed each tear away tenderly. "What is it, darling? You can tell *me*."

"Oh, I want to tell you, Dan. I want to, but I don't dare! Things are so nice just the way they are. I don't want anything to change."

"Nothing has to change."

Linda shook her head in despair. "You wouldn't say that if you knew. You don't understand."

He smiled, as though to say, "But I do."

She closed her eyes. It was easier to tell secrets that way. "I'm going to have a baby, Daniel. Yours and mine. A little . . . baby." She burst into tears again, but this time Daniel did not, tenderly, kiss them away.

"But how . . . ?" he asked.

"I knew it. I knew you'd be angry. Oh, I should never have told you. Don't look at me that way, Daniel."

He ventured a weak smile. "Are you positive? Have you been to a doctor?"

"Not yet—but a woman knows these things. I've known for three months."

Daniel had nothing more to say. After a little while he helped her up from the bench and walked with her to the brownstone apartment on West 88th where she lived. He didn't go up the stairs with her as he usually did. Instead he kissed her good night in the lobby, by the mailboxes. He had never seemed so handsome to Linda as he did on that night.

That was the last time that Linda saw Daniel.

The next day, on her lunch hour, Linda went to see Dr.

Theo Fingal, a gynecologist whose name she had found in the Yellow Pages. The doctor's waiting room was as cheerful and intimate as if it had been a room in his own house, and gradually, under its influence, Linda began to feel less nervous. She passed the time by reading Dr. Spock's book.

The receptionist asked Linda what her name was.

"Lee," she said. "Linda Lee."

Mrs. Linda Lee, the receptionist wrote on a white card.

"Not Mrs.," Linda explained painfully. "Miss."

The receptionist didn't bat an eyelid. She led Linda into a little room, as cheerless as the waiting room had been pleasant, and told her to undress, the doctor would be with her in a minute. She obeyed reluctantly. No man had ever seen her undressed before, except for Daniel, which wasn't the same thing.

But when Dr. Fingal came to examine her, he spoke to her as though he hadn't even noticed her nudity, even making little jokes. He was consideration itself. He could touch her, and it was as though no one had touched her at all. After the examination, a blood sample, and X-rays, he told her to put her clothes on and come back in three days. He said everything was for the best and there was nothing to worry about.

Nevertheless, she couldn't help worrying. She could scarcely sleep the next three nights. She took long walks, alone, in the park. At the office, she reversed the carbons of letters she was typing on three separate occasions.

When she returned on the appointed day, Dr. Fingal was very upset. "Sit down, Mrs. Lee," he said with exaggerated solicitude. "What I have to say will come as something of a shock."

"Not Mrs.," she explained. "Miss."

"This is a terrible thing," said the doctor, fingering the white card before him nervously.

Linda bit her lip. "Well, I know *that,* Doctor, or I wouldn't have come to see you."

"It's not what you think, Miss Lee. I assume that you have been under the impression that you are pregnant. Am I correct?"

Linda nodded.

"I'm afraid it's a more serious matter than that. I'm afraid you have cancer."

Linda gasped, clutching at her stomach, as though the

Linda and Daniel and Spike

doctor had struck the child growing in her womb. "No! That isn't true!"

"It is malignant," Dr. Fingal continued ruthlessly, "and surgery will be necessary within two months. After that time, metastasis—or the spreading of the cancerous cells throughout the body—will almost certainly occur. However, there is every reason to believe that the operation will be a success, since we have nipped it, as it were, in the bud."

"You mean . . . an abortion?" she asked, horror stricken.

The doctor looked at her curiously. "I'm afraid you haven't understood me, Miss Lee. This isn't a baby. This is uterine cancer."

Linda slapped him in the face, knocking his glasses to the floor. While he bent down to retrieve them, Linda grabbed up the card with her name and address on it, and walked out of the office. There was still half an hour left of her lunch period, so she went to a nearby Chinese restaurant and ordered Moo Goo Gai Pan.

"I'm all alone now," she said to herself, but even as the bitter words fell from her lips, she could feel the new life stirring in her womb and she knew that they were not, quite, true.

Linda was delivered of child in her tenth month—or, in a more clinical sense, the tumor metastasized. The labor was terrible, but when it was over and the nurse had brought in the little darling, tears of pure happiness welled from Linda's eyes.

It was a boy.

"I shall call him Spike," Linda told the nurse.

"Spike?" the nurse asked. "Nothing more than that?" She had been under the impression that Linda was a Catholic.

"That was his father's name," she explained. "He's so big, isn't he?"

"Twenty-two pounds," the nurse confirmed. "Almost a record for this hospital."

"And so very red! Are they always so red at first?"

The nurse, whose shift was almost over, ignored Linda's question. If you let them, mothers will spend all day talking about their little bastards. "I have to take him back to his crib now, Miss Lee."

Linda kissed her little cancerbaby, and the nurse took him away. "Spike," Linda whispered to herself. "Spike, my little Spike."

Spike grew very quickly. He was up to Linda's knees, to her hips, to her ribs in seemingly no time at all. He was not what you would have called a handsome child—but Linda, naturally, was blind to that. She doted on him. As soon as he was big enough to be put into a day school, she found work again. She would have preferred, for her own part, to keep on Welfare, but it was hard to feed Spike on the pittance the city provided. In the evening she stayed at home, alone, with Spike.

Even before he had learned to talk, she had read books to him—books about science, about the theater, about politics. She knew how important a good education was nowadays, and she was determined that he would have one. Spike, for his own part, showed an incredible appetite for learning. As soon as he was old enough for his own library card, he began to choose his own books. She couldn't understand half of them. After he had gone to bed, she would sit in the bathroom (the light in the kitchen would keep him awake) and read the books over again with uncomprehending admiration, softly pronouncing the words she did not understand: unilateral, carcinoma, masque, retribution . . .

She was never able to discuss the books with him though, as she had once discussed things with Daniel, for Spike was taciturn and kept to himself. Once, in fact, when he was eleven and really too old for such behavior, he bit the postman who had just brought his mother a special delivery letter.

"Who can it be from?" she wondered aloud. Her parents had died two years ago, and there was no one else who would have written to her by special delivery.

It was from Spike!

In the letter Spike explained how, although he was taciturn and kept to himself, he loved her, his mother, very much and would always be grateful for the endless sacrifices she had made for him, always, even when she was dead. All that he was and all that he ever hoped to be, he explained, he owed to his darling mother. The extravagance of his language made Linda blush.

"What a lovely letter!" Linda exclaimed aloud in her son's hearing. But Spike pretended to take no heed. *He's*

Linda and Daniel and Spike

embarrassed, she thought. *He doesn't want to admit how deep his feelings are for me.* This trait was common in children of his age, according to Dr. Spock. Linda decided to say nothing more about it.

She didn't have the heart, that night, to scold him about having bitten the postman. Though she knew that she was spoiling him, she didn't care. Secretly, in fact, she wanted to spoil him. It seemed to bring them closer together.

At about this time Spike began stealing from his mother. He took only small sums at first, but one Sunday morning she woke to discover that Spike had left the house, taking the coinpurse with everything in it. This time she did scold him.

"What are we going to *do* now?" she asked, with strident emphasis. "What shall we eat for *food?*"

Spike hung his head without speaking. Not really, she suspected, out of shame, but because there was no answer to such a question.

"Answer me! Look me in the eye!" She took his face in her hands, and though she was angry it was not a rough gesture. He bit her hand.

To prevent him stealing from her purse she gave him a weekly allowance of $15. He spent most of his money on clothing. Since he was now six foot seven inches tall, he had a hard time finding good ready-made clothing. Linda would have liked to have made his clothing for him, but he wouldn't allow her to do that. He stayed out till all hours. He reminded Linda, at times, of his father, especially the way he would, at times, half in jest and half in earnest, bite her. Once, when he was fifteen, he bit her thumb off, and she had to go to the hospital.

At the hospital she had a room all by herself and fresh flowers every day. Spike didn't visit her (visiting hours were during school), but he did send the loveliest get-well card. He had made it himself with colored paper and aluminum foil. The poem inside was of his own composition. It was more the kind of poem that a boy would write to his girl-friend than to his own mother. It made Linda blush.

The doctor said, "Yes, yes, Mrs. Lee—just a little while longer. Everything is looking up."

"But I must really be getting back. My son is there all alone, with no one to look after him."

"Your son, yes. How old is he, Mrs. Lee?"

"Fifteen. This is the get-well card he sent me. Have you seen it?"

The doctor examined the get-well card.

"He made it himself," Linda explained proudly.

She told the nurses, too, about him: how he knew everything there was to know about science, the theater, politics. She told them some of the names of the books he read. Even their names made no sense. "I wish you could meet him," she would usually conclude with a sigh. "He's *very* handsome. You'd have to watch *out* for him, or he'd sweep you off your feet."

Then they took her to the operating room. She explained, blushingly, that it was impossible for her to have *another* baby. She hadn't been with a man for over fifteen years. Of course Spike was a man now, altogether a man, but he was her son.

"Where is his get-well card?" she said. "I'll show you that."

The nurse pretended to go to her room to look for the imaginary get-well card.

The original tumor was found to have metastasized to every part of the body. Separate tumors were removed from the lungs, the breasts, the larynx, the liver, the lymph glands, and the brain, not to mention the original tumor in the uterus. The largest tumor weighed fully five pounds; their total combined weight was sixty-four pounds, rather better than half of her original body weight. It was a record not only for the hospital, but for medical science.

The nearest of kin, the woman's son, was informed, and he ordered the remains to be cremated, though not, at the hospital's request, the tumors. These are still on display.

Flight Useless, Inexorable the Pursuit

As he stumbled against the hedge, a car passed, brushing his face with its cruel light. The hedge trembled all along its length, like a large molded gelatin, and for minutes after the rimed and sickly leaves quivered. Thighs quivered. He ought not to run, but his terror ... Consciously, he walked down the street of identical Tudor houses. 48, 46, 44, 42, 40, 38, never skipping a beat. Before some of the houses, the dozen or so square yards of lawn had been stripped away and replaced with asphalt or concrete. They had become miniature parking lots. The cold air performed surgeries in his lungs. He had lost his gloves, or forgotten them when he'd left the house. How long ago? The thing had caught sight of him returning from the bakery. The bag of jelly doughnuts was probably still where he had set it down, on the dinette table growing stale. At seven, or maybe eight P.M. Now it was dark again. A night and a day gone by. Thinking of the doughnuts, he grew hungry though it was a false hunger: he had eaten several times during the day—sandwiches from delicatessens, teas and pastries at Lyons shops, sixpenny bags of crisps. Until his money had run out. He ought to have taken a train out of London at the start. Instead he'd squandered his money shuttling about town. Always when he stopped—in Stepney, in Bethnal Green, in Camden Town, it found him out. How did it track him? How had it known *at first?* Not, he was certain, by his face. Admittedly he was quite pale, but in London, in winter, most people are pale. Did it, perhaps, affect the way he walked? No—scent seemed the only way to account for it. His pursuer had smelled him out, like a truffle; it hunted him, as a hound a hare. 24, 22, 20, 18, 16. 16 was FOR SALE.

He had only been to Temple Fortune once before, when he had been searching so desperately for a flat. He had looked at a rather commodious bedsitter on Ashbourne Avenue, but that had not been possible, as he would have had to share the bath. He had, even yet, more conscience than that. Could someone have seen him getting in or out of the tub at Portland Road, and reported it? Not, one would have supposed, with a window of frosted glass. And at work he never used the toilets, out of the same consideration. London lacked the customary air of *suspicion* of a Marrakesh or a Beirut. He must escape, he *had* to escape. Escape where? Back to Portland Road to pack? But what if one of those things were waiting there? In the closet. No, it would never have fit in the closet. Somewhere else. No, the risk was too great. He should have thought, during the day, to go to his bank. Too late. He shivered, remembering again its metronomic knock, remembered looking out the paranoid peephole he'd drilled in the door the day he'd moved in. Lucky that he had! Remembered the gray low bulk of it, like nothing so much as an overturned icebox. How had it got up stairs? Did it walk—or, which seemed likelier, use treads? He knew almost nothing of its capabilities. Was its seeming sluggishness a ruse? So that when it finally came close enough it could make a sudden, unanticipated spurt? He must escape but he was so tired. Two days and a night without sleep. He had to rest, but he dared not rest. He would cross the Channel and go north. To Denmark. Then Sweden. He would always be able to find some kind of light work. His chest hurt. He had never dared visit a London doctor with his cold, even at its worst. No matter what medicines he took, it lingered on. It was the cold that made him so giddy now, not ... the other thing. The cold and fear. Fear and weariness, a terrible weariness, so that he dared not even stand in a doorway and rest his eyes. He would have slept and the machine would have tracked him down, inexorably. Where would it be now? Somewhere along the Finchley Road, no doubt, sniffing after him the way he'd come on the bus. He'd reached the corner of the block, a greengrocer's, and, opposite, a dairy that was just closing. And here he had thought the time nearly midnight! He squinted at the street sign above the greengrocer's awning. This was the corner of Finchley Road and Ashbourne Avenue. He'd come full circle on himself! The light in the dairy was switched off. He leaned back against the cold glass of the greengrocer's door and stared at the car parked before him, its windows opaque with frost. It had been such a warm winter until just this week, and he had been grateful for that, since he was unable, now, to wear woollen clothes. His chest hurt and his legs hurt. He crossed the street and walked down Finchley Road until he found a turning to the left. He turned left. He walked past rows and rows of identical Tudor houses, and in each of them lived an identical Tudor king. He was hungry, he needed to sleep, and his chest hurt. He would go to Sweden, though he couldn't speak Swedish. Someone had told him that every Swede spoke English as a second language. He knew Arabic though, for all the good that would do him! How had they let him get through Customs? To have come so far, to have come so close, and now ... The street ended, and there was nothing but a vacancy. Had he come as far south as the Heath? A hill, trees. The sky's underbelly, livid with electric light. Soon, with the new mirrors being orbited, London would be bathed in an eternal day. The birds would stay awake all through the night, flowers would forget to close their blossoms. He remembered the devastated slopes of the Atlas mountains, the maddened villagers. He was leaning against the trunk of a tree, sheltered by the bare branches. The joint between his skull and the upper vertebrae ached and creaked as though in need of lubrication. He allowed his eyes to close. He had known all along really that his flight was useless. Already at the foot of the hill he saw it—an overturned icebox. It approached at an even, slow speed over the frozen ground, following exactly the path he had taken. It had come this close in Camden Town, and yet he had escaped it then. He could still ... No. Just as a suicide will undress before entering the water, he unbuttoned his overcoat and let it slip from his shoulders. The machine paused two feet from him. One motor ceased its purring, another sprang to life, but there was, between these sounds, a brief, hallowed silence. The blunt forepart of the machine began to lift up, and he thought he could see, through the grid that covered it, tiny electric lights flickering within. When it was fully upright, it was a foot and a half shorter than him. The telescoping limbs began to strip away his cotton suit, quickly but with gentleness. The protective plates slid aside to reveal the main compartment, and for the first time he could see its huge rubber lips. Then, inexorably, the rubber lips kissed the leper's open sores.

Descending

Catsup, mustard, pickle relish, mayonnaise, two kinds of salad dressing, bacon grease, and a lemon. Oh yes, two trays of ice cubes. In the cupboard it wasn't much better: jars and boxes of spice, flour, sugar, salt—and a box of raisins!

An empty box of raisins.

Not even any coffee. Not even tea, which he hated. Nothing in the mailbox but a bill from Underwood's: *Unless we receive the arrears on your account . . .*

$4.75 in change jingled in his coat pocket—the plunder of the Chianti bottle he had promised himself never to break open. He was spared the unpleasantness of having to sell his books. They had all been sold. The letter to Graham had gone out a week ago. If his brother intended to send something this time, it would have come by now.

—I should be desperate, he thought.—Perhaps I am.

He might have looked in the *Times*. But, no, that was too depressing—applying for jobs at $50 a week and being turned down. Not that he blamed them; he wouldn't have hired himself himself. He had been a grasshopper for years. The ants were on to his tricks.

He shaved without soap and brushed his shoes to a high polish. He whitened the sepulchre of his unwashed torso with a fresh, starched shirt and chose his somberest tie from the rack. He began to feel excited and expressed it, characteristically, by appearing statuesquely, icily calm.

Descending the stairway to the first floor, he encountered Mrs. Beale, who was pretending to sweep the well-swept floor of the entrance.

"Good afternoon—or I s'pose it's good morning for you, eh?"

"Good afternoon, Mrs. Beale."

"Your letter come?"

"Not yet."

"The first of the month isn't far off."

"Yes indeed, Mrs. Beale."

At the subway station he considered a moment before answering the attendant: One token or two? Two, he decided. After all, he had no choice, but to return to his apartment. The first of the month was still a long way off.

—If Jean Valjean had had a charge account, he would have never gone to prison.

Having thus cheered himself, he settled down to enjoy the ads in the subway car. *Smoke. Try. Eat. Live. See. Drink. Use. Buy.* He thought of Alice with her mushrooms: Eat me.

At 34th Street he got off and entered Underwood's Department Store directly from the train platform. On the main floor he stopped at the cigar stand and bought a carton of cigarettes.

"Cash or charge?"

"Charge." He handed the clerk the laminated plastic card. The charge was rung up.

Fancy groceries was on 5. He made his selection judiciously. A jar of instant and a 2-pound can of drip-ground coffee, a large tin of corned beef, packaged soups and boxes of pancake mix and condensed milk. Jam, peanut butter, and honey. Six cans of tuna fish. Then, he indulged himself in perishables: English cookies, and Edam cheese, a small frozen pheasant—even fruitcake. He never ate so well as when he was broke. He couldn't afford to.

"$14.87."

This time after ringing up his charge, the clerk checked the number on his card against her list of closed or doubtful accounts. She smiled apologetically and handed the card back.

"Sorry, but we have to check."

"I understand."

The bag of groceries weighed a good twenty pounds. Carrying it with the exquisite casualness of a burglar passing before a policeman with his loot, he took the escalator to the bookshop on 8. His choice of books was determined by the same principle as his choice of groceries. First, the staples: two Victorian novels he had never read, *Vanity Fair* and *Middlemarch*; the Sayers' translation of Dante, and a two-volume anthology of Ger-

Descending

man plays none of which he had read and few he had even heard of. Then the perishables: a sensational novel that had reached the best seller list via the Supreme Court, and two mysteries.

He had begun to feel giddy with self-indulgence. He reached into his jacket pocket for a coin.

—Heads a new suit; tails the Sky Room.

Tails.

The Sky Room on 15 was empty of all but a few women chatting over coffee and cakes. He was able to get a seat by a window. He ordered from the à la Carte side of the menu and finished his meal with Espresso and baklava. He handed the waitress his credit card and tipped her fifty cents.

Dawdling over his second cup of coffee, he began *Vanity Fair*. Rather to his surprise, he found himself enjoying it. The waitress returned with his card and a receipt for the meal.

Since the Sky Room was on the top floor of Underwood's there was only one escalator to take now—Descending. Riding down, he continued to read *Vanity Fair*. He could read anywhere—in restaurants, on subways, even walking down the street. At each landing he made his way from the foot of one escalator to the head of the next without lifting his eyes from the book. When he came to the Bargain Basement, he would be only a few steps from the subway turnstile.

He was halfway through Chapter VI (on page 55, to be exact) when he began to feel something amiss.

—How long does this damn thing take to reach the basement?

He stopped at the next landing, but there was no sign to indicate on what floor he was nor any door by which he might re-enter the store. Deducing from this that he was between floors, he took the escalator down one more flight only to find the same perplexing absence of landmarks.

There was, however, a water fountain, and he stooped to take a drink.

—I must have gone to a sub-basement. But this was not too likely after all. Escalators were seldom provided for janitors and stockboys.

He waited on the landing watching the steps of the escalators slowly descend toward him and, at the end of their journey, telescope in upon themselves and disappear.

He waited a long while, and no one else came down the moving steps.

—Perhaps the store has closed. Having no wristwatch and having rather lost track of the time, he had no way of knowing. At last, he reasoned that he had become so engrossed in the Thackeray novel that he had simply stopped on one of the upper landings—say, on 8—to finish a chapter and had read on to page 55 without realizing that he was making no progress on the escalators.

When he read, he could forget everything else.

He must, therefore, still be somewhere above the main floor. The absence of exits, though disconcerting, could be explained by some quirk of the floor plan. The absence of signs was merely a carelessness on the part of the management.

He tucked *Vanity Fair* into his shopping bag and stepped onto the grilled lip of the down-going escalator—not, it must be admitted, without a certain degree of reluctance. At each landing, he marked his progress by a number spoken aloud. By *eight* he was uneasy; by *fifteen* he was desperate.

It was, of course, possible that he had to descend two flights of stairs for every floor of the department store. With this possibility in mind, he counted off fifteen more landings.

—No.

Dazedly and as though to deny the reality of this seemingly interminable stairwell, he continued his descent. When he stopped again at the forty-fifth landing, he was trembling. He was afraid.

He rested the shopping bag on the bare concrete floor of the landing, realizing that his arm had gone quite sore from supporting the twenty pounds and more of groceries and books. He discounted the enticing possibility that "it was all a dream," for the dream-world is the reality of the dreamer, to which he could not weakly surrender, no more than one could surrender to the realities of life. Besides, he was not dreaming; of that he was quite sure.

He checked his pulse. It was fast—say, eighty a minute. He rode down two more flights, counting his pulse. Eighty almost exactly. Two flights took only one minute.

He could read approximately one page a minute, a little less on an escalator. Suppose he had spent one hour on the

Descending

escalators while he had read: sixty minutes—one hundred and twenty floors. Plus forty-seven that he had counted. One hundred sixty-seven. The Sky Room was on 15.

167—15=152.

He was in the one-hundred-fifty-second sub-basement. That was impossible.

The appropriate response to an impossible situation was to deal with it as though it were commonplace—like Alice in Wonderland. Ergo, he would return to Underwood's the same way he had (apparently) left it. He would walk up one hundred fifty-two flights of down-going escalators. Taking the steps three at a time and running, it was almost like going up a regular staircase. But after ascending the second escalator in this manner, he found himself already out of breath.

There was no hurry. He would not allow himself to be overtaken by panic.

No.

He picked up the bag of groceries and books he had left on that landing, waiting for his breath to return, and darted up a third and fourth flight. While he rested on the landing, he tried to count the steps between floors, but this count differed depending on whether he counted with the current or against it, down or up. The average was roughly eighteen steps, and the steps appeared to be eight or nine inches deep. Each flight was, therefore, about twelve feet.

It was one-third of a mile, as the plumb drops, to Underwood's main floor.

Dashing up the ninth escalator, the bag of groceries broke open at the bottom, where the thawing pheasant had dampened the paper. Groceries and books tumbled onto the steps, some rolling of their own accord to the landing below, others being transported there by the moving stairs and forming a neat little pile. Only the jam jar had been broken.

He stacked the groceries in the corner of the landing, except for the half-thawed pheasant, which he stuffed into his coat pocket, anticipating that his ascent would take him well past his dinner hour.

Physical exertion had dulled his finer feelings—to be precise, his capacity for fear. Like a cross-country runner in his last laps, he thought single-mindedly of the task at hand and made no effort to understand what he had in any case already decided was not to be understood. He mounted one flight, rested, mounted and rested again. Each mount was wearier; each rest longer. He stopped counting the landings after the twenty-eighth, and some time after that—how long he had no idea—his legs gave out and he collapsed to the concrete floor of the landing. His calves were hard aching knots of muscle; his thighs quivered erratically. He tried to do knee-bends and fell backward.

Despite his recent dinner (assuming that it had been recent), he was hungry and he devoured the entire pheasant, completely thawed now, without being able to tell if it were raw or had been pre-cooked.

—This is what it's like to be a cannibal, he thought as he fell asleep.

Sleeping, he dreamed he was falling down a bottomless pit. Waking, he discovered nothing had changed, except the dull ache in his legs, which had become a sharp pain.

Overhead, a single strip of fluorescent lighting snaked down the stairwell. The mechanical purr of the escalators seemed to have heightened to the roar of a Niagara, and their rate of descent seemed to have increased proportionately.

Fever, he decided. He stood up stiffly and flexed some of the soreness from his muscles.

Halfway up the third escalator, his legs gave way under him. He attempted the climb again and succeeded. He collapsed again on the next flight. Lying on the landing where the escalator had deposited him, he realized that his hunger had returned. He also needed to have water—and to let it.

The latter necessity he could easily—and without false modesty—satisfy. Also he remembered the water fountain he had drunk from yesterday and he found another three floors below.

—It's so much easier going down.

His groceries were down there. To go after them now, he would erase whatever progress he had made in his ascent. Perhaps Underwood's main floor was only a few more flights up. Or a hundred. There was no way to know.

Because he was hungry and because he was tired and because the futility of mounting endless flights of descending escalators was, as he now considered it, a labor of Sisyphus, he returned, descended, gave in.

At first, he allowed the escalator to take him along at its own mild pace, but he soon grew impatient of this. He found that the exercise of running down the steps three at a time was not so exhausting as running *up*. It was refreshing, almost. And, by swimming with the current instead of against it, his progress, if such it can be called, was appreciable. In only minutes he was back at his cache of groceries.

After eating half the fruitcake and a little cheese, he fashioned his coat into a sort of a sling for the groceries, knotting the sleeves together and buttoning it closed. With one hand at the collar and the other about the hem, he could carry all his food with him.

He looked up the descending staircase with a scornful smile, for he had decided with the wisdom of failure to abandon *that* venture. If the stairs wished to take him down, then down, giddily, he would go.

Then, down he did go, down dizzily, down, down and always, it seemed, faster, spinning about lightly on his heels at each landing so that there was hardly any break in the wild speed of his descent. He whooped and halooed and laughed to hear his whoopings echo in the narrow, low-vaulted corridors, following him as though they could not keep up his pace.

Down, ever deeper down.

Twice he slipped at the landings and once he missed his footing in mid-leap on the escalator, hurtled forward, letting go of the sling of groceries and falling, hands stretched out to cushion him, onto the steps, which, imperturbably, continued their descent.

He must have been unconscious then, for he woke up in a pile of groceries with a split cheek and a splitting headache. The telescoping steps of the escalator gently grazed his heels.

He knew then his first moment of terror—a premonition that there was no *end* to his descent, but this feeling gave way quickly to a laughing fit.

"I'm going to hell!" he shouted, though he could not drown with his voice the steady purr of the escalators. "This is the way to hell. Abandon hope all ye who enter here."

—If only I were, he reflected.—If that were the case,

it would make sense. Not quite orthodox sense, but some sense, a little.

Sanity, however, was so integral to his character that neither hysteria nor horror could long have their way with him. He gathered up his groceries again, relieved to find that only the jar of instant coffee had been broken this time. After reflection he also discarded the can of drip-ground coffee, for which he could conceive no use—under the present circumstances. And he would allow himself, for the sake of sanity, to conceive of no other circumstances than those.

He began a more deliberate descent. He returned to *Vanity Fair*, reading it as he paced down the down-going steps. He did not let himself consider the extent of the abyss into which he was plunging, and the vicarious excitement of the novel helped him keep his thoughts from his own situation. At page 235, he lunched (that is, he took his second meal of the day) on the remainder of the cheese and fruitcake; at 523 he rested and dined on the English cookies dipped in peanut butter.

—Perhaps I had better ration my food.

If he could regard this absurd dilemma merely as a struggle for survival, another chapter in his own Robinson Crusoe story, he might get to the bottom of this mechanized vortex alive and sane. He thought proudly that many people in his position could not have adjusted, would have gone mad.

Of course, he *was* descending . . .

But he was still sane. He had chosen his course and now he was following it.

There was no night in the stairwell, and scarcely any shadows. He slept when his legs could no longer bear his weight and his eyes were tearful from reading. Sleeping, he dreamed that he was continuing his descent on the escalators. Waking, his hand resting on the rubber railing that moved along at the same rate as the steps, he discovered this to be the case.

Somnambulistically, he had ridden the escalators further down into this mild, interminable hell, leaving behind his bundle of food and even the still-unfinished Thackeray novel.

Stumbling up the escalators, he began, for the first

time, to cry. Without the novel, there was nothing to *think* of but this, this ...

—How far? How long did I sleep?

His legs, which had only been slightly wearied by his descent, gave out twenty flights up. His spirit gave out soon after. Again he turned around, allowed himself to be swept up by current—or, more exactly, swept down.

The escalator seemed to be traveling more rapidly, the pitch of the steps to be more pronounced. But he no longer trusted the evidence of his senses.

—I am, perhaps, insane—or sick from hunger. Yet, I would have run out of food eventually. This will bring the crisis to a head. Optimism, that's the spirit!

Continuing his descent, he occupied himself with a closer analysis of his environment, not undertaken with any hope of bettering his condition but only for lack of other diversions. The walls and ceilings were hard, smooth, and off-white. The escalator steps were a dull nickel color, the treads being somewhat shinier, the crevices darker. Did that mean that the treads were polished from use? Or were they designed in that fashion? The treads were half an inch wide and spaced apart from each other by the same width. They projected slightly over the edge of each step, resembling somewhat the head of a barber's shears. Whenever he stopped at a landing, his attention would become fixed on the illusory "disappearance" of the steps, as they sank flush to the floor and slid, tread in groove, into the grilled baseplate.

Less and less would he run, or even walk, down the stairs, content merely to ride his chosen step from top to bottom of each flight and, at the landing, step (left foot, right, and left again) onto the escalator that would transport him to the floor below. The stairwell now had tunneled, by his calculations, miles beneath the department store—so many miles that he began to congratulate himself upon his unsought adventure, wondering if he had established some sort of record. Just so, a criminal will stand in awe of his own baseness and be most proud of his vilest crime, which he believes unparalleled.

In the days that followed, when his only nourishment was the water from the fountains provided at every tenth landing, he thought frequently of food, preparing imaginary meals from the store of groceries he had left behind, savoring the ideal sweetness of the honey, the richness of the soup which he would prepare by soaking the powder in the emptied cookie tin, licking the film of gelatin lining the opened can of corned beef. When he thought of the six cans of tuna fish, his anxiety became intolerable, for he had (would have had) no way to open them. Merely to stamp on them would not be enough. What, then? He turned the question over and over in his head, like a squirrel spinning the wheel in its cage, to no avail.

Then a curious thing happened. He quickened again the speed of his descent, faster now than when first he had done this, eagerly, headlong, absolutely heedless. The several landings seemed to flash by like a montage of Flight, each scarcely perceived before the next was before him. A demonic, pointless race—and why? He was running, so he thought, toward his store of groceries, either believing that they had been left *below* or thinking that he was running *up*. Clearly, he was delirious.

It did not last. His weakened body could not maintain the frantic pace, and he awoke from his delirium confused and utterly spent. Now began another, more rational delirium, a madness fired by logic. Lying on the landing, rubbing a torn muscle in his ankle, he speculated on the nature, origin and purpose of the escalators. Reasoned thought was of no more use to him, however, than unreasoning action. Ingenuity was helpless to solve a riddle that had no answer, which was its own reason, self-contained and whole. He—not the escalators—needed an answer.

Perhaps his most interesting theory was the notion that these escalators were a kind of exercise wheel, like those found in a squirrel cage, from which, because it was a closed system, there could be no escape. This theory required some minor alterations in his conception of the physical universe, which had always appeared highly Euclidean to him before, a universe in which his descent seemingly along a plumb-line was, in fact, describing a loop. This theory cheered him, for he might hope, coming full circle, to return to his store of groceries again, if not to Underwood's. Perhaps in his abstracted state he had passed one or the other already several times without observing.

There was another, and related, theory concerning the measures taken by Underwood's Credit Department against delinquent accounts. This was mere paranoia.

Descending

—Theories! I don't need theories. I must get on with it.

So, favoring his good leg, he continued his descent, although his speculations did not immediately cease. They became, if anything, more metaphysical. They became vague. Eventually, he could regard the escalators as being entirely matter-of-fact, requiring no more explanation than, by their sheer existence, they offered him.

He discovered that he was losing weight. Being so long without food (by the evidence of his beard, he estimated that more than a week had gone by), this was only to be expected. Yet, there was another possibility that he could not exclude: that he was approaching the center of the earth where, as he understood, all things were weightless.

—Now *that*, he thought, is something worth striving for.

He had discovered a goal. On the other hand, he was dying, a process he did not give all the attention it deserved. Unwilling to admit this eventuality and yet not so foolish as to admit any other, he side-stepped the issue by pretending to hope.

—Maybe someone will rescue me, he hoped.

But his hope was as mechanical as the escalators he rode—and tended, in much the same way, to sink.

Waking and sleeping were no longer distinct states of which he could say: "Now I am sleeping," or "Now I am awake." Sometimes he would discover himself descending and be unable to tell whether he had been waked from sleep or roused from inattention.

He hallucinated.

A woman, loaded with packages from Underwood's and wearing a trim, pillbox-style hat, came down the escalator toward him, turned around on the landing, high heels clicking smartly, and rode away without even nodding to him.

More and more, when he awoke or was roused from his stupor, he found himself, instead of hurrying to his goal, lying on a landing, weak, dazed, and beyond hunger. Then he would crawl to the down-going escalator and pull himself onto one of the steps, which he would ride to the bottom, sprawled head foremost, hands and shoulders braced against the treads to keep from skittering bumpily down.

—At the bottom, he thought—at the bottom ... I will ... when I get there ...

From the bottom, which he conceived of as the center of the earth, there would be literally nowhere to go but up. Probably another chain of escalators, ascending escalators, but preferably by an elevator. It was important to believe in a bottom.

Thought was becoming as difficult, as demanding and painful, as once his struggle to ascend had been. His perceptions were fuzzy. He did not know what was real and what imaginary. He thought he was eating and discovered he was gnawing at his hands.

He thought he had come to the bottom. It was a large, high-ceilinged room. Signs pointed to another escalator: *Ascending*. But there was a chain across it and a small typed announcement.

"Out of order. Please bear with us while the escalators are being repaired. Thank you. The Management."

He laughed weakly.

He devised a way to open the tuna fish cans. He would slip the can sideways beneath the projecting treads of the escalator, just at the point where the steps were sinking flush to the floor. Either the escalator would split the can open or the can would jam the escalator. Perhaps if one escalator were jammed the whole chain of them would stop. He should have thought of that before, but he was, nevertheless, quite pleased to have thought of it at all.

—I might have escaped.

His body seemed to weigh so little now. He must have come hundreds of miles. Thousands.

Again, he descended.

Then, he was lying at the foot of the escalator. His head rested on the cold metal of the baseplate and he was looking at his hand, the fingers of which were pressed into the creviced grille. One after another, in perfect order, the steps of the escalator slipped into these crevices, tread in groove, rasping at his fingertips, occasionally tearing away a sliver of his flesh.

That was the last thing he remembered.

Nada

"What word begins with *J?*" Oveta Wohlmuth surveyed the twenty apathetic faces confronting her, the forty dull eyes that watched her only because the seats in the classroom did not comfortably allow them to focus on anything else. "Jill—"

Jill Coldfax looked down at the maple slab of her desk, stolidly silent, invincibly ignorant, resigned and resentful.

"*J*—can't you think of a word that begins with a *J*-sound, Jill?"

Three children laughed; Oveta, for the moment ignored them. The remaining sixteen faces had sunk, weighted by shame, to contemplate the varnished surfaces of their desks, where, as in mirrors, they were confronted with their own natures: blank tablets upon which years of abuse had left a few beautiless scars as the only evidence of their passage—sixteen faces thus, except for one, which stared at Oveta with disconcerting steadiness, avoiding her glance; which had stared at her so all that day and for many days past.

"Nada—what begins with *J?*"

Nada had been gazing at the monogram on Oveta's collar. Since she had been moved, in November, to the front row (where it was harder to go to sleep) Nada Perez had learned to achieve trance state without even closing her eyes.

"Nada!"

"Kangaroo. *K* is for Kangaroo."

"We are on *J*, Nada." For all that, it was a kind reproach.

"I thought you asked that already. *J* is for Jam." Nada's eyes slipped back from the ironic twist of Oveta's lip to the soothing nothingness of the silver O.

"And what is a kangaroo?"

Nobody knew. She sketched one on the blackboard and pointed out Australia on the Repogle globe, but the forty eyes rested on these artifacts of their education with the same glazed and weighty disinterest that they had evidenced for anything that came before them in the guise of learning.

These children were the special problems in a school for the exceptional: special in the sense that all the other teachers there had despaired of them. All, that is, except Oveta Wohlmuth, who, partly because they were her job and partly because it was natural to her, was more optimistic. "I *can* teach them to learn," she had said once to a friend, once her fiancé, now only a colleague, a specialist himself in exceptional children—but exceptional for their talent rather than their lack of it.

"Why bother?" he had scoffed. "So that they can, after great labors, achieve something less than mediocrity?"

"Why ever bother, John? I bother because others won't, because someone must."

Sometimes, fortunately, it was worth her bother. Sometimes she would break through the apathy, see light dawning in eyes suddenly alive, watch the first floods of knowledge wash across the shallows of a retarded face. At such moments she could have answered her doubters more eloquently. Many years ago there had been Alfredo, who had become an Air Force officer and was occasionally mentioned in news accounts of Pentagon intrigues; and, more recently Marion, who had married an orthodontist and was raising three dismayingly bright children. They, and their like, were the reasons she could not stop bothering, although she was now past fifty and, with her doctorate and years of experience with "special problems," could easily have retired to the relative ease of college teaching. That she did two evenings a week.

Now there was Nada.

A very special problem, Nada. The girl knew much that she would not admit to knowing: the alphabet, words like kangaroo. Oveta suspected that the real limits of her clandestine knowledge were far broader than her few accidental betrayals of it could lead one justly to believe. In fact, she suspected that Nada was a genius-in-hiding, and, like a hunter close on the scent, she was excited at the prospect of scaring that genius out of cover.

But Nada was a difficult quarry. She could be relentlessly, stupefyingly dull. Only once that Oveta had seen had Nada forgotten to be dull. It had been during art period, the day the class had tried watercolors. While the other nineteen special problems wrestled unhappily with the special problems of watercolor, Nada painted. She *painted*.

A picture of the gray Brooklyn tenements outside the schoolroom, not distorted into forbidding expressionistic shapes, but quietly real; full volumes in true spaces—beautiful. It reminded Oveta somehow of a seascape: the elemental rhythms of the calligraphy, the subdued colors, its peace.

So it was that that afternoon—the Day of the Kangaroo—Oveta asked Nada to stay after class. Nada stood before the teacher's desk, a dowdy twelve-year-old, fat, sallow, her clothes in need of laundering, her black hair hanging down to her shoulders in untended, greasy curls, dark eyes staring with steady, dull fixity on Oveta's silver pin.

"How do you feel you're coming along in school, Nada?" The girl shifted her weight with lethargic uneasiness. "I mean ... you don't seem to take an interest in classwork. Perhaps it bores you?"

"No."

"Do you like school?"

"Yes, I like school."

"What do you like about it?" Oveta asked shyly.

"I—" Nada's mouth hung open as though she were waiting for Oveta to fill it with words she could not invent herself. Then, when the words did not come, it slowly closed.

"Do you like art class? You do very nice things, you know. With a little practice you could become a good painter. Would you like that?"

"I—" Then, slowly, it closed.

"Of course, practice is important. Do you practice at home?"

"No."

"Would you like to?"

"Yes ... " An uncertain yes, but for all that, Oveta had made her say it.

"Here, then, is a set of watercolor paints, and here is some special paper. The paints belong to the school, so take good care of them."

They lay in Nada's hands, like alien artifacts demanding explication.

"You can take them home—to practice with. Now run along, darling, and show me what you've done, tomorrow."

Oveta never called a child darling.

"A spaceship?" Mrs. Butler asked.

"Well, it didn't look quite like a spaceship," Oveta went on. "It was shaped a little more like a cornucopia."

"Do you still have the picture?"

"No, Nada took it back home with her."

"How would she know the exact dimensions of a spaceship?" Butler asked in a rhetorical tone. "Or anyone else, for that matter? Especially a twelve-year-old retarded Puerto Rican girl. Or, even if she had some idea from TV or the movies, her draftsmanship might not have been up to the job."

"Her draftsmanship is excellent. Judge for yourself; there's an example hanging in your living room."

In the living room at that moment there was a shiver of minor-keyed music, a voice that cried: *"But don't you understand? Earth is being invaded!"*

"Turn down the volume, Billy," Butler shouted into the living room. Then, turning back to Oveta: *"She did that!—* and I thought at first glance it was a Marin! Mmm. Is your plan working out with her?" A tone of professional interest had crept into his voice. "Is she doing better in school?"

"Not that I can see."

"Martians!" said the voice in the next room. *"Now I've heard everything!"*

"Don't be discouraged," Mrs. Butler said with perfunctory good cheer. "Would you like another piece of pie?"

"Thank you, no."

"There they are now—coming out of the sewers!"

"Would you tell Billy to turn down the TV," Butler shouted. "You can't hear yourself think. Oveta, that girl is *talented*. She'll waste away in that slum, marry some dock worker, and never be seen again if we don't do something for her—and soon."

"Billy, turn off the TV and come and have another piece of pie."

"Oh, how horr—"

Oveta smiled. "That's why I came to see you."

"Why does she have this block against learning anything? I've heard of geniuses camouflaging as average kids—but as a sub-normal?"

"Where is it?" Billy asked, taking his place at the table. His mother handed him the pie.

"She's a very strange girl," Oveta said. "I don't understand her at all."

"A pretty girl?" Mrs. Butler asked.

"On the contrary, quite unattractive. She lives with her mother; no father is mentioned on her enrollment card . . ."

Mrs. Butler tssked. "And the mother's on relief, I suppose."

"I suppose," Oveta grudged. "A slum background. No books in the home. She probably didn't learn English till she came to school. It's not unusual."

"She's unusual, though," Butler insisted.

"Dad, do Martians have tentacles?"

"Don't interrupt the grown-ups, Billy," Mrs. Butler scolded. "And don't be silly—there's no such thing as Martians."

"He's only asking a question, Bridget. And we don't know there aren't any Martians. When we land a spaceship on Mars, Billy," he explained, "we'll find out whether there are Martians—and if they have tentacles."

"On TV," Billy explained patiently, "they showed one. It wasn't on Mars. It was in the sewer, and it had tentacles and big eyes . . ."

"That was just a story. They weren't the *real* Martians," Mrs. Butler added sarcastically, for her husband's benefit.

". . . and they were going to conquer Earth," Billy concluded.

"Martians are a much-maligned people," Oveta said with mock seriousness. "Always the invaders. If I were a Martian, I think I'd settle down and take it easy."

Butler's eyes twinkled. "Like Mrs. Perez?" he suggested.

"Yes," Oveta twinkled. "Like Mrs. Perez." Mrs. Butler's cooking was beginning to have its usual effects. She felt the first spasm of indigestion.

"If you folks will excuse me, it's time I started on my way home."

"Watch out for the Martians!" Billy shouted to her

when she reached the door. Billy doubled with laughter. His father chuckled.

Outside, the air was misty—verging on rain. Oveta raised the hood of her coat.

—Is it too late to go there? she wondered. As though there were ever really a proper time for it!

Once already that week, when Nada had shown her the watercolor of the odd, cornucopean spaceship (starship, she had called it) circling above the distant, moonlit Earth and then had returned the watercolors and left the classroom with a mumbled "Thanks," Oveta had given way to an unconsidered impulse and followed the girl home. Just to see, she had told herself, what Nada's neighborhood was like. She had kept a block's distance between her and her quarry, careful of the film of ice that slicked the streets, preventing herself from thinking of anything but the mechanics of pursuit and concealment; on her right hand, an unending, undifferentiated facade of brick and brownstone, on her left, a monotonous procession of parked cars or, sometimes, banks of soot-crusted snow; and Nada always a block ahead.

She had been too ashamed of her senseless pursuit of Nada to mention it to Butler that evening. She was still ashamed—and upset—remembering Nada's face at the moment before she had gone up the brownstone steps and into the tenement building, glancing back, not even *looking,* but knowing that Oveta was there and viewing her as casually as if she had been only a part of the landscape. With neither special recognition nor surprise, simply knowing Oveta was there and then turning away, while Oveta's face had crimsoned and blanched with shame.

Now, as the shame of remembering ebbed away again, Oveta climbed into her gray Renault (thinking again that her legs were really too long for a compact car), and set off in the direction of the waterfront.

It was nine forty-five. The drive, from Butler's apartment toward the waterfront, took her half an hour. She stopped the car by a candy store one block from Nada's building. It had begun to rain.

—In general, the evidence for telepathy is very slight, she thought, while, on the other side of rationality, her mind conjured up the image of a large-eyed, tentacled Martian. (If I were a Martian, she remembered saying, and then Billy's laughter, his father's chuckle: *Watch out for them!*) She pulled her cloth coat more tightly about her and set off against the wind that siphoned up the street from the East River.

By the time she reached 1324, Nada's address, she was chilled through. It was a narrow, six-floor walk-up, with a facade identical to five other buildings in the row. The half-flight of brownstone steps that projected from the doorway onto the sidewalk had been painted bilge-green, a color much-favored by Brooklyn landlords. The green shone with incandescent fervor in the light of the street-lamp overhead. Oveta hesitated at the foot of the stairs.

An old woman trundling a baby carriage passed on the sidewalk and stopped before the row of garbage cans stuffed full of the morning's collection beside the entrance way to 1324. She rummaged through the refuse, oblivious of Oveta, and fished out three nylon stockings knitted into a ball and a broken umbrella. These she put in the carriage and trundled on to the next hoard.

"Starlight, starbright, hope to see a ghost tonight!"

Across from 1324 was an asphalt lot, pretending with a few metal poles to be a playground, from which three small figures ran now, pell-mell, giggling.

"Ready or not, here I come."

It was *almost* Nada's voice. Oveta couldn't be sure. Hesitantly, she crossed the narrow ill-lit street. The girl who was *it* couldn't be seen now. Oveta thought she heard from *somewhere* a child's giggle.

"Nada?" she called out uncertainly.

The rain was now a steady drizzle that seemed to hang stationary in the air, haloing the street-lamps with coronas of cold, blue light. Across the street in 1324 Oveta saw the silhouette of a fat woman in a third floor window. As she watched it, it moved out of sight.

"Nada, are you here?"

"Lousy weather," a voice behind her piped. Turning to see who had addressed her, she became aware that her coat was soaked through.

"But not so bad for January." He chuckled, as though it were the punch line of a joke, the rest of which he had forgotten or did not need to recount. A man's voice, though high-pitched, and wearing a man's clothes, but not the figure of a man. Sitting in the swing (a child's swing that adult hips could not have squeezed into), his feet dangled inches from the asphalt. A midget—or a dwarf. Oveta could not decide, for the swing lay in the shadow of the adjacent building.

"I don't recognize your face. New in the neighborhood?"

"Yes. I mean—a visitor."

"Thought so. I know most of the faces on this street. I used to live over there ... " he waved his hand in a vague arc. ". . . over there," he echoed himself. ". . . and I couldn't help overhearing you mention Nada. You know her?"

"Yes, I do."

"Nice girl. Make a good wife for some lucky fellow." He chuckled.

"Do *you* know Nada?" Oveta asked overeagerly, for the little man made her feel uncomfortable, afraid that he might think she patronized him.

"Nice girl," he repeated.

"You've spoken with her?"

"Well, she doesn't have much to say—you know how it is. Women aren't great talkers."

"No," Oveta agreed reluctantly, for her experience had led her to the opposite conclusion.

"Men are the talkers. Men will make plans, have the big ideas, reach for the stars. Talking, all the time, like me."

She smiled, as a practical measure to keep her teeth from chattering. "Spaceships are certainly a man's idea," she volunteered.

"But it's the women," he went on, beginning to rock back and forth in the enclosing seat of the swing, "that get things done. From day to day. Practical. A woman."

In the awkward interval of silence that ensued, broken only by the squeakings of the swing and the susurrus of the rain (which had become heavier, falling in distinct droplets on her cheeks), Oveta stood to leave.

"Nada," the little man began, and ended.

"Nada?" Oveta questioned. The momentum of the swing had died out. His head hung slumped onto his chest. "Are you all right?"

"I'm fine. It's nice weather for January. The rain. I pretend it's warm."

"Could I take you home?"

"I don't have a home."

"I'm sorry. To a hotel somewhere, then? I could loan you a little money. The rain isn't really warm."

"My wife, you know," he continued, ignoring her offer, perhaps not even hearing it, "my wife died."

"I'm sorry."

"Well, that's the way the tide rises." He chuckled.

Slowly Oveta retreated toward the street, stepping backward, her eyes on the man, whose hands now fell limply off the sidebars of the swing. When she reached the sidewalk, she turned.

There was only one light on in 1324, in a third-floor window. Even in silhouette, she could recognize Nada, and she imagined her eyes, dull, impassive, and knowing, offering no recognition, as though Oveta were no more than a figure in a landscape of her own invention.

"She *knows*," Oveta whispered. She began to run.

In the car, she discovered that she had lost one of her shoes on the street, and she had to wait several minutes before her hand was steady enough to insert the ignition key.

"You mean you've *never* been in Manhattan before?"

"No," Nada repeated, "never."

"Amazing! Why, you're a pure specimen of the Brooklynite. I sometimes think that I've been parochial. . . . Do you know what parochial means?"

"It's a kind of school, but you mean narrow-minded, don't you?"

Oveta laughed. "The opposite of cosmopolitan—or international. And speaking of that—those are the United Nations buildings on your right. Are you interested in architecture?"

"No. I mean—it doesn't seem necessary. Nobody needs a building like that to live in."

"Nobody needs paintings for that matter."

"True."

Oveta was inebriated with her success. The hunt was over; her quarry had broken cover, and she would never be able to return to her pose of numbed stupidity—Oveta would see to that.

That morning, Saturday, Oveta had awakened with the beginnings of a cold and the conviction that she would never be able to speak to Nada again. For exactly that reason she had resolved to return to 1324 on the pretext of taking Nada to the Metropolitan Museum, a visit that Nada had once lukewarmly agreed to make. An unannounced visit to a student's home and then her virtual abduction were not professional tactics, but Oveta had convinced herself that, unless she openly declared herself to Nada, the girl would forever distrust her. Since Nada knew already she was being hunted, Oveta had to tell her *why*.

The plan worked smoothly. Nada had been delivered over to her abductress without the least fuss. Of Mrs. Perez, Oveta had seen only one suspicious eye when she had opened the door and a fat-wreathed forearm thrusting Nada outside. As soon as they had got into the Renault, Oveta had declared: "You know, Nada, I think you are probably a very intelligent girl and I think you're trying to hide it."

And Nada had replied without hesitation: "I know. I know you thought that." And then shrugged. But, ever so slightly, she had been smiling. Her eyes had not yet been glazed with their customary dullness but had examined the car with curiosity. "I've never been in one of these before," she had said, the first time, to Oveta's knowledge, she had ever spoken without being addressed a question.

"In a Renault, you mean?"

"In a car. Does it go?" Nada was smiling.

"Yes, it goes."

"The Metropolitan Museum," Nada had said dreamily. "Well, well . . ."

"Well, here it is, Nada: the Metropolitan Museum. How do you like it?"

"It's too big: it's ugly!"

"Don't judge a book by its cover."

"Why, Miss Wohlmuth, I don't judge books at all."

Oveta laughed, until she began to choke. Her cold was growing worse. "That must change," she brought out weakly, as they mounted the museum steps.

Nada pouted. Each new expression on the girl's face astonished Oveta, as though she were witnessing a prodigy of nature. She didn't feel entirely in control of the situation (as she had with Alfredo or Marion), but it was more exciting that way.

They hesitated in the Grand Hall, dwarfed by colossal Corinthian columns. Oveta felt awed by the sheer size of the space enclosed by the columns; unconsciously she began to breathe more deeply. Nada, on the other hand, seemed altogether unaffected.

"The paintings are on the second floor, and over to your right are the Egyptian rooms. Hieroglyphics, big basalt statues, and part of a pyramid, a small one. Even so, you'd probably find it all too oversized for your tastes."

"Oh, but I like the Egyptians. They never changed— their art, the way they lived. If it hadn't been for other people coming in, interfering, they would always have stayed the same."

"I suppose we're all like that."

"Let's see the paintings."

Nada gave one glance at the Renaissance paintings and snorted with contempt. Only once in these rooms did Nada show enthusiasm to any degree—for Crivelli's *Madonna and Child*. It was also a favorite of Oveta's.

"Look at the fly on the ledge—the shadow it casts," Oveta pointed out.

"Mmm . . . No, what *I* like is the thing hanging up at the top, by the apples. Its shape. What is it, some kind of vegetable?"

"Squash, I think," Oveta answered crestfallen. "Or maybe a cucumber. The draftsmanship is beautiful, isn't it? Look at the Virgin's fingers, the curve of her wrist."

"Oh, but that's so *easy!*"

"You try it. You'll see how easy it is."

"What I mean is, it's already been done. Everything here has already been done. Why should I try to do something that's already been done?"

Like a witness going down the line-up at the police station, Nada was hurried past the accumulated centuries of painting. There was little that aroused her interest. Bruegel's *Harvesters* inspired her to say respectfully, "It makes you feel sort of sleepy," but her response to Rosa Bonheur's *Horse Fair* reawakened Oveta's worst fears. *The Horse Fair* was a large, furious painting of horses rearing and plunging and galloping on an arc that seemed to sweep out of the picture-plane toward the spectator. One could almost hear the shouting, the stomping, the neighing of the horses, the wind of their running.

"How awful!" Nada gasped.

"Why awful?"

"Oh, it's just too—I mean everything is going somewhere: It makes me dizzy. And a *woman* painted it!"

"Rosa Bonheur, about a century ago. How did you know?" They were standing several feet back from the huge canvas, and at that distance the nameplate was illegible.

"I—" Her mouth hung open, waiting for the words to fill it. Oveta grew frightened, recognizing the characteristic expression of insensibility that was stealing over Nada's features: jaws slackened, eyes fixed on a void, the flesh of her face utterly relaxed, inert.

"Shall we get something to eat? Nada! Listen to me! Would you like to eat now? Shall we go to the restaurant I told you about?"

"Yes."

In the museum restaurant, Nada regained some degree of alertness by being forced to select a pastry from the rack. By the time she had finished eating it, she seemed fully recovered, and Oveta relaxed again. She had let her coffee go cold before her, tasted once and set aside. Her throat was sore and dry, but the coffee's steaming bitterness repelled her. It's coming along nicely, she thought: I'll be in bed with a cold tomorrow.

"Well, I'm surprised at you, Nada," she said with forced cheer. "I thought you'd find a few Old Masters, at least, who could measure up to your standards. Your tastes seem to be pretty solidly formed."

"Not at all. I've never thought about painting before. But I *do* like the Flemish painters better than the Italian ones. Their women have better shapes."

(—Like squash, Oveta thought.) She said, "That's a pretty definite taste, it seems to me. Where do you learn all the things you know? You must do a lot of reading."

"I *can't* read. You know that. Isn't it time to go home?"

"It's still early, Nada. Would you like to take a walk through the park? We could see Cleopatra's Needle and get some fresh air. And it's only a short way to the Planetarium."

"To see the stars, you mean?"

"Yes. The stars."

"No, that would be . . . boring." She yawned for emphasis.

"Are you tired?"

"Yes. Let's go home."

Last night's rain had frozen to the streets, and Oveta had to divide her attention between Nada and the mechanics of driving. Twice Nada fell asleep, only to be awakened when the car skidded uncertainly to a stop at icy street corners. Oveta manufactured commonplace conversation, pointing out the buildings along Fifth Avenue: St. Patrick's ("No," Nada said, "I don't go to church."); the Library ("No, I don't have a card."); and the Empire State Building ("How awful!").

Finally Oveta blurted out the question she had meant to introduce off-handedly, at an appropriate moment, but that moment had never come. "What are you going to do when you grow up, Nada?"

"Oh—get married, I guess."

"Do you have any boy-friends yet?" Oveta asked doubtfully.

"Mmmm." Nada snuggled into the chill plastic upholstery.

"But don't you want anything *else?* Painting, or some kind of job?"

"No."

"Nothing else at all?"

"No. Nothing. It's cold in here, don't you think?"

"We're almost home now. Do you suppose I could stop in for a moment to have a cup of coffee? It is, as you say, cold in here. Something must be wrong with the heater."

"I guess so," Nada said, with grave doubt.

"If it's too much trouble . . ."

"No. You can come in."

"And in good time! Here we are . . . 1324."

Standing in the garlic-weighted hallway, while Nada negotiated with her mother to let her into the apartment, Oveta listened to the chirruping and trills of what seemed to be a whole aviary of canaries in the apartment opposite the Perez'.

Nada came to the door. "Just a minute. Mommy wants to clean up."

"Don't hurry." But Nada had already disappeared into the apartment. Down the hallway, Oveta watched a fat woman with a shopping bag full of groceries labor up the narrow stairway to the next floor, stopping at every third step for breath. Over the trilling of the canaries Oveta could hear the strained tones of Nada's mother, tugging at something and uttering Spanish imprecations.

"Come in." (—And in good time, Oveta thought.)

"Thank you." She offered her hand to Mrs. Perez, who regarded it as though she saw through the flesh to a particularly unwholesome tumor. "I'm so glad to meet you at last, Mrs. Perez."

"No hablo Inglés."

"She can't speak English," Nada interpreted.

Oveta repeated her lukewarm amenity in Spanish: *"Mucho gusto de concerla, Señora Perez."* Mrs. Perez turned her back on Oveta to throw a pile of unlaundered clothes from an armchair to the unswept floor. Cockroaches scuttered from the heap.

"Yeah," Mrs. Perez said, "the same to you. Have a chair."

"Why—thank you." Oveta repressed her scruples and sat in the threadbare armchair. There might be bugs, but she could take a bath later, at home.

"You wanna drink?"

"Just a cup of—a drink? Whatever you're having. Thank you."

"Nada, get some glasses."

While Nada went into the next room, her mother sat down on a mattress on the floor and stared at Oveta, who was herself staring at the room in which she found herself, like a Dowager Queen touring her dungeons, suddenly trapped. Oveta could not imagine what measures of tidying Mrs. Perez had taken with the room, for it seemed in a nearly perfect state of disorder: clothes, blankets, and what seemed no more than rags, in various conditions of dirtiness, were heaped over and stuffed under the few scant pieces of furniture. The walls were a pastiche of wallpapers (Oveta counted four distinct patterns) and green paint in various stages of discoloration. The patchwork of linoleum and bare boards on the floor presented a similar spectacle, like an uncared-for billboard in the warehouse district from which the rains had peeled the years' detritus of posters irregularly to create a ragged montage of meaninglessness. Yet, the final impression was not one of wild disarray, or even of untidiness, but rather, sedative, asleep, like a garden gone to seed.

Perhaps it was the figure of Mrs. Perez that produced that impression, for her figure certainly dominated the room. She was a gargantuan woman, of vast breasts and a stomach that hung, gothic and pendulous, over the edge of the mattress and rested on a patch of bare, unpainted boards. It was her face that most fascinated Oveta, for it was the nightmare image of the face that Nada's could become: devoid of expression, stuporous, and vaguely, almost obscenely sensuous, like a composite allegory of the more lethargic vices.

Nada handed her mother three grease-clouded tumblers, which the woman filled brim-full with gin. (Oveta presumed it was gin; the bottle, which she replaced at the side of the mattress, was unlabeled.) One tumbler she handed to Oveta, one she kept for herself, the last was Nada's. Oveta sipped warily at her drink; it was gin. Nada drank from her glass as though it contained, at the worst, a sweetened medicine.

Outrageous! Oveta thought. But she kept the thought to herself.

"Mud in your eye!" Mrs. Perez mumbled into her glass, which she proceeded to drain in two swallows and a switch of her tongue.

"Cheers," Oveta returned.

A smile faded from Nada's lips. Her eyes began to take on the glazed, benign indifference of her mother's.

"Nada has told me so much about you," Oveta lied.

"Yeah, kids talk too much."

"Really? I've always thought her a very *quiet* girl. Until today," she added, smiling at Nada, who lowered her eyes to stare at her tumbler of gin and seemed to blush.

"Whadya say?" Mrs. Perez poured herself another tumblerful.

"Nothing. Nothing at all."

"Mud in your eye."

"Cheers," Oveta replied gloomily, taking a sip of gin. Actually, the liquor felt good trickling down her sore throat, but she felt that she would lose any advantage she possessed in Nada's eyes by seeming to enjoy it.

"Nice apartment."

"Like hell," Mrs. Perez said.

"I beg your pardon?"

"Like hell," Nada repeated. "But I think it's a nice apartment too. Mommy's joking."

Mrs. Perez no longer made a pretense of sitting up. She

lay back on the mattress, her eyes closed and began to snore.

"Your mother seems to be quite . . . worn out."

"She's always that way."

Only a few rays of the afternoon's dying light penetrated the grime-coated windows to spend their power dimly and to no purpose upon the montage of floor and walls and heaped clothing; darkness spread over the room like a rising tide.

"Nada," Oveta whispered, "you don't want *this*." Her hands gestured awkwardly, but her tone conveyed her disgust eloquently. "You can't. Nada, let me help you get away from this."

"But, I do."

"Nada, please."

"This *is* what I want. I *like* it."

Mrs. Perez rolled over on the mattress. "Get out of here," she grunted. "Go on, get out."

When Oveta reached the door, she imagined she heard a chuckle, high-pitched and mocking, but she realized it was only the canaries trilling in the next apartment.

Oveta Wohlmuth's living room was untidy. It could never have been called untidy before, but now there was no other word for it.

Oveta had been in bed (or on the sofa) for four days with her cold. Saturday evening, after returning home in a high fever, she had had to call in a doctor. Sunday she could not remember at all, and the rest of the week until today she had spent impatiently convalescing from what threatened constantly to become pneumonia. Breathing was still slightly painful. Coughing was an agony, but holding it back was worse agony. The doctor had been strict: she could not leave her apartment.

She had contented herself with phoning the substitute teacher twice a day. Nada had not come to school on Monday, or on Tuesday, or yesterday, or today. Perhaps, Oveta thought, Nada had caught cold too, but it was a very faint *perhaps*. The school nurse had visited 1324 and claimed that she couldn't find the Perez apartment.

Oveta had made another series of phone calls while she was confined to her apartment, breathing in the medicated fumes that steamed out of the vaporizer. She had called Butler and social workers she knew and, by force of will and patient and repeated explanations, had extorted from them the papers she would need to remove Nada temporarily from her mother. Temporarily—while that woman was tried for incompetence and a number of other charges that Oveta had not too closely inquired of. She had also persuaded the welfare agency to allow her to call for Nada, when the legal process had been completed. Now she was waiting for Butler to arrive with those papers.

To pass the time, she made a few ineffectual gestures of housecleaning, but she quickly exhausted herself and ended up on the sofa, fighting to regain her breath. Butler found her not quite recovered.

"Are you sure you're well enough to leave the house?"

"Positive. Now, help me on with my coat, will you? God, I still feel so *guilty!* It's my first legal kidnapping. Usually, I'm against meddling."

"From what you told me about Mrs. Perez . . ."

"I know. But I still feel guilty. It's irrational."

In Butler's car, with a traveling blanket over her legs, she pulled the hood of her coat close about her fever-reddened face. Butler could see the trembling of her hands even beneath the bulky fur mittens.

"Oveta, if you're too sick—"

"Damn the sickness! We've got a job to do. Now let's get on with it."

The car pulled away from the curb. Oveta kept glancing to Butler's face and away; several times her lips parted to speak. Then, hesitatingly, she began: "When I was sick, John, I couldn't help thinking about Nada. I couldn't read. My eyes would begin to smart, and my mind would wander. I kept thinking of Nada.

"I was sick. I'm still sick, for that matter. What I mean to say is, I don't really *believe* what I'm going to tell you . . . No that's not true either. The commonplace, commonsense Miss Wohlmuth doesn't believe it, but, I think *I* do. At least, it's *possible*—and that's bad enough."

Butler made a *moue* of impatience. "Get to the point."

"Well, then. Imagine a race, John—an alien race, telepathic, living on another planet, in another part of the galaxy. Imagine that they have spaceships—no, starships. They've traveled everywhere, seen everything—or enough to satisfy them that they've seen all they need to. Telepaths can share their knowledge. What one has known and seen, they all know and remember. Their minds are filled with it: knowledge memories, piling up through the generations."

"A dismal picture," Butler commented

"So dismal that they might decide just to blot it out."

"You're shivering, Oveta."

"And you're trying to humor me. Just listen for a minute. Nada is such an alien. She's telepathic. I've seen that for myself. And I've already told you about that starship she painted, drawn, probably, from a memory in her mother's mind. And her attitude, her uncanny quiescence—her background—can't be explained in any other way."

"You explained it well enough another way—gin."

"No, let me finish. Mrs. Perez is not human: she doesn't look human or act human. She's a vegetable on two feet. She has only one purpose in life: homeostasis, physiological equilibrium, Nirvhana. She eats, she drinks, she sleeps, she breeds more vegetables, and that's all she wants out of life. A Homeostat. There are thousands more like her, and God only knows how many of them are . . ."

Butler laughed indulgently. "It's a nice theory. It fits the facts. But a simpler theory will fit the facts just as well."

"It doesn't fit the way I feel about Nada—and Nada's mother."

"Look, Oveta—you've been sick, and that scene with Mrs. Perez upset you. We all feel uneasy about the Mrs. Perezes of this world. She's a Homeostat, as you put it, and she's turning Nada into another. That doesn't mean she's an alien telepath, for God's sake."

"Women," Oveta went on dreamily, "*women* are more likely to be vegetables, you know. Squash and cucumbers. I'll tell you something else. It was explained to me by a widower of my acquaintance, but I didn't understand him at the time. They are married to little men—midgets. It was the men who built the spaceships in the first place, but the women got their way in the end, when the men were ready to give up, when they'd seen all there was to see, when their minds were filled up until they couldn't hold any more."

"So they came to Earth to go on relief?" Butler asked mockingly.

"Because it was the easiest thing to do. They could

leave the shell of their own civilization behind. It was too much trouble to keep it intact, and they only wanted homeostasis after all. Well, they've got it."

"Oveta, if I didn't know you better, I'd think you'd cracked under the strain."

"That's why I told you and not someone else. I know it's a theory for the casebooks, but when I lay in bed thinking of Nada, all the pieces began to lock together, by themselves. I feel like the victim of my own idea. It's not just for Nada's sake that I want to get her out of the nightmare she's living in. At the hospital, they're bound to discover any—anomalies. I hope I'm wrong, but if there are aliens ... " Oveta began to cough, a lung-ripping cough that brought the conversation to an abrupt end.

"1324," Butler announced, as they stood before the door of the tenement, "where two civilizations meet. Do you think you can get up the steps?"

"I'll make it." On the second floor landing, where she was attacked by another fit of coughing, she was almost proven wrong.

In the third floor hallway, the lights were dim, the air heavy with garlic, and the canaries were still to be heard. "You knock," she asked Butler. "I feel slightly *déjà vu*."

The door was answered by a woman Oveta had never seen before. She was very fat; her eyes were dull. "Perez? Perez don't live here any more."

"Where have they moved? It's very important that we know."

"I dunno. They just *moved*. Away."

"But *where?*" The door was closed in Oveta's face.

Her eyes burned with an intensity: of fear; of sickness; of understanding too well. "We *won't* find her new address either. Did you see her? She was one of them. I could tell. They knew I'd come back for Nada. I must have been thinking about it when I left them and they read my mind."

Behind them, down the hall, there was the patter of a child's steps ascending the stairway.

"Now I'll never find out. They've won!"

"Oveta, be reasonable. Mrs. Perez didn't need telepathy to figure you'd be back. Oveta? Oveta, for God's sake, what's the matter!"

A boy edged by them in the hallway and entered what

had been the Perez apartment. He was not quite three feet tall, and he wore a mustache.

Oveta had fainted.

Then she was outside again, and the weather seemed milder than it had a minute ago. Children were playing in the asphalt lot, and down the street Oveta recognized the old woman with the baby carriage.

"Are you all right, darling?"

Oveta smiled at the unfamiliar tenderness, then, remembering what she had just seen, the smile stiffened into a rictus of terror. "That midget in the hall. Did you see him? He had a mustache."

"That was just a boy—just a little boy. His mustache was probably painted on. Little boys will do that." He rested his hand on her brow.

"You've helped me so much, John. I don't know how to thank you."

"Oveta, look—in the ashcan. Isn't that an art pad?"

"Do you think—?"

Butler removed the tablet of watercolor paper from the garbage pail and shook off the coffee grounds that covered it. A drawing fell out.

"The spaceship," they said in chorus. And, indeed, it was the spaceship, poised, above the hazy globe of Earth, at the instant before its descent, like an enormous apple just caught in the grip of Newton's Laws.

"Is there anything else?" Oveta asked, hoping there was, and hoping, as well, against it.

Butler opened the pad and grew numb, as before a basilisk.

"Let me see!"

"It doesn't mean anything. A child's imagination. Nothing ... "

Oveta grabbed the watercolor pad.

Underneath the picture, in an almost illegible scrawl, Nada had penciled the words: MOMMY AND DADDY.

The woman was recognizably "Mrs. Perez." Nada had captured perfectly the stuporous expression, the ponderous weight of the breasts and abdomen. Of the man, only his face was visible: eyes twinkling with an ageless wisdom and unwanted knowledge, an ironic smile on his thin lips. The rest of him—his dwarf's body—was nestled securely in Mrs. Perez's marsupial pouch.

Now Is Forever

Charles Archold liked the facade best at twilight. On June evenings like this (Was it *June?*), the sun would sink into the canyon of Maxwell Street and spotlight the sculptured group in the pediment: a full-breasted Commerce extended an allegorical cornucopia from which tumbled allegorical fruits into the outstretched hands of Industry, Labor, Transportation, Science, and Art. He was idling past (the Cadillac engine was beginning to misfire again, but where could you find a mechanic these days?), abstractedly considering the burning tip of his cigar, when he observed peripherally that Commerce had been beheaded. He stopped.

It was against the law; a defacement, an insult. Maxwell Street echoed the slam of the car door, his cry—"Police!" A swarm of pigeons rose from the feet of Industry, Labor, Transportation, Science and Art and scattered into the depopulated streets. The bank president achieved a smile of chagrin, although there was no one in sight from whom he would have had to conceal his embarrassment. Archold's good manners, like his affluent paunch, had been long in forming and were difficult to efface.

Somewhere in the acoustical maze of the streets of the financial district Archold could hear the rumble of a procession of teenage maenads approaching. Trumpets, drums, and screaming voices. Hurriedly, Archold locked his car and went up the bank steps. The bronze gates were open; the glass doors were unlocked. Drapes were drawn across the windows as they had been on the day, seven months earlier or thereabouts, when he and the three or four remaining staff members had closed the bank. In the gloom, Archold took inventory. The desks and office equipment had been piled into one corner; the carpets had been torn up from the parquet floor; the tellers' cages had been arranged into a sort of platform against the back wall. Archold flicked on a light switch. A spotlight flooded the platform with a dim blue light. He saw the drums. The bank had been converted into a dancehall.

In the sub-basement, the air-conditioner rumbled into life. Machines seemed to live a life of their own. Archold walked, nervously aware of his footsteps on the naked parquet, to the service elevator behind the jerry-built bandstand. He pressed the UP button and waited. Dead as a doornail. Well, you couldn't expect everything to work. He took the stairs up to the third floor. Passing through the still plush reception room outside his office, he noticed that there were extra couches along the walls. An expensive postermural representing the diversified holding of the New York Exchange Bank had been ripped from the wall; a gargantuan and ill-drawn pair of nudes reclined where the mural had been. Teenagers!

His office had not been broken into. A thick film of dust covered his bare desk. A spider had constructed (and long ago abandoned) a web across the entire expanse of his bookshelves. The dwarf tree that stood in a pot on the window sill (a present, two Christmases ago from his secretary) had shriveled into a skeleton where, for a time, the spider had spun other webs. An early model Reprostat (of five years ago) stood beside the desk. Archold had never dared to smash the machine, though, God knew, he had wanted to often enough.

He wondered if it would still work, hoping, of course, that it would not. He pressed the Archtype button for memo pad. A sign flashed red on the control panel: INSUFFICIENT CARBON. So, it worked. The sign flashed again, insistently. Archold dug into one of his desk drawers for a bar of carbon and fed it into the hopper at the base of the Reprostat. The machine hummed and emitted a memo pad.

Archold settled back in his own chair, raising a cloud of dust. He needed a drink or, lacking that (he drank too much, he remembered) a cigar. He'd dropped his last cigar in the street. If he were in the car, he could just touch a button, but here ...

Of course! His office Reprostat was also set to make his own brand of cigars. He pressed the cigar Archtype button; the machine hummed and emitted one Maduro cigar, evenly burning at its tip. How could you ever be angry with the machines? It wasn't their fault the world was in a shambles; it was the fault of people that misused the machines—greedy, shortsighted people who didn't care what happened to the Economy or the Nation as long as they had Maine lobster every day and a full wine cellar and ermine stoles for a theater opening and . . .

But could you blame them? He had himself spent thirty years of his life to get exactly those things or their equivalents, for himself—and for Nora. The difference was, he thought as he savored the usual aroma of his cigar (before the Reprostats, he had never been able to afford this brand. They had cost $1.50 apiece, and he was a heavy smoker)—the difference was simply that some people (like Archold) could be trusted to have the best things in life without going haywire, while other people, the majority, in fact, could not be trusted to have things that they couldn't pay for with their own industry. It was now a case of too many cooks. Authority was disappearing; it had vanished. Morality was now going fast. Young people, he had been informed (when he still knew people who would tell him these things), didn't even bother to get married any more—and their elders, who should have set them an example, didn't bother to get divorced.

Absent-mindedly, he pressed the Reprostat button for another cigar, while the one he had been smoking lay forgotten in the dusty ashtray. He had argued with Nora that morning. They had both been feeling a little under the weather. Maybe they had been drinking again the night before—they had been drinking quite a lot lately—but he could not remember. The argument had taken a bad turn, with Nora poking fun (and her finger) at his flabby belly. He had reminded her that he got his flabby belly working all those years at the bank to provide her with the house and her clothes and all the other expensive obsolescing goodies she could not live without.

"Expensive!" she had screamed. "What's expensive any more? Not even money is expensive."

"Is that *my* fault?"

"You're fifty years old, Charlie boy, *over* fifty, and I'm still young," (she was forty-two, to be exact) "and I don't have to keep you hanging around my neck like an albatross."

"The albatross was a symbol of guilt, my dear. Is there something you're trying to tell me?"

"I wish there was!"

He had slapped her, and she had locked herself in the bathroom. Then he had gone off for a drive, not really intending to come past the bank, but the force of habit had worked upon his absent-minded anger and brought him here.

The office door edged open.

"Mr. Archold?"

"Who!—oh, Lester, come in. You gave me a start."

Lester Tinburley, the former janitor-in-chief of the Exchange Bank, shambled into the office, mumbling reverent how-do-you-do-sirs and nodding his head with such self-effacing cordiality that he seemed to have palsy. Like his former superior (who wore a conservative gray suit, fresh that morning from the Reprostat), Lester wore the uniform of his old position: white-and-blue striped denim overalls, faded and thin from many launderings. The black peppercorn curls of his hair had been sheared down to shadowy nubbins. Except for some new wrinkles in the brown flesh of his face (scarcely noticed by Archold), Lester appeared to be in no way different from the janitor-in-chief that the bank president had always known.

"What's happened to the old place, Lester?"

Lester nodded his head sadly. "It's these kids—you can't do a thing with them nowadays. All of them gone straight to the devil—dancing and drinking and some other things I couldn't tell you, Mr. Archold."

Archold smiled a knowing smile. "You don't have to say another word, Lester. It's all because of the way they were raised. No respect for authority—that's their problem. You can't tell them anything they don't know already."

"What's a person going to do, Mr. Archold?"

Archold had the answer even for that. "Discipline!"

Lester's palsy, as though Archold had given a cue, became more pronounced. "Well, I've done what I could to keep things up. I come back every day I can and look after things. Fix up what I can—what those kids don't smash up for their own fun. All the records are in the basement now."

"Good work. When things return to normal again, we'll

have a much easier job, thanks to you. And I'll see that you get your back wages for all the time you've put in."

"Thank you, sir."

"Did you know that someone has broken the statue out in front? The one right over the door. Can't you fix it somehow, Lester? It looks just terrible."

"I'll see what I can do, sir."

"See that you do." It was a good feeling for Archold, giving orders again.

"It is sure good to have you back here, sir. After all these years ... "

"Seven months, Lester. That's all it's been. It does seem like years."

Lester glanced away from Archold and fixed his gaze on the skeleton of the dwarf tree. "I've been keeping track with the calendars in the basement, Mr. Archold. The ones we stocked for '94. It's been two years and more. We closed April 12, 1993 ... "

"A day I'll never forget, Lester."

"... and this is June 30, 1995."

Archold looked puzzled. "You've gotten confused, boy. It couldn't be. It's ... it *is* June, isn't it? That's funny. I could swear that yesterday was Oct ... I haven't been feeling well lately."

A muffled vibration crept into the room. Lester went to the door.

"Maybe you'd best leave now, Mr. Archold. Things have changed around the old bank. Maybe you wouldn't be safe here."

"This is my office, my bank. Don't tell *me* what to do!" His voice cracked with authority like a rusted trumpet.

"It's those kids. They come here every night now. I'll show you out through the basement."

"I'll leave the way I came, Lester. I think you'd better return to your work now. And fix that statue!"

Lester's palsy underwent a sudden cure, his lips tightened. Without another word or a look back, he left Archold's office. As soon as he found himself alone, Archold pressed the Beverage, alcoholic Archtype button on the Reprostat. He gulped down the iced Scotch greedily, threw the glass into the hopper and pressed the button again.

At midnight Jessy Holm was going to die, but at the

moment she was deliriously happy. She was the sort of person that lives entirely in the present.

Now, as every light in the old Exchange Bank was doused (except for the blue spot on the drummer), she joined with the dancing crowd in a communal sigh of delight and dug her silvered fingernails into Jude's bare arm.

"Do you love me?" she whispered.

"Crazy!" Jude replied.

"How much?"

"Kid, I'd die for you." It was true.

A blat of static sounded from the speakers set into the gilded ceiling of the banking floor. In the blue haze about the bandstand, a figure swayed before the microphone. A voice of ambiguous gender began to sing along to the hard, rocking beats of the music—only noises it first seemed; gradually, a few words emerged:

> *Now, now, now, now—*
> *Now is forever.*
> *Around and around and around—*
> *Up and down*
> *And around and around—because*
> *Tonight is forever*
> *And love, lo-ove is now.*

"I don't want to stop, ever," Jessy shouted above the roar of the song and the tread of the dancers.

"It's never gonna stop, baby," Jude assured her. "C'mon let's go upstairs."

The second floor lobby was already filled with couples. On the third floor they found themselves alone. Jude lit cigarettes for himself and Jessy.

"It's scary here, Jude. We're all alone."

"That's not gonna last long. It's getting near ten o'clock."

"Are you scared—about later, I mean?"

"Nothing to be scared of. It doesn't hurt—maybe for just a second, then it's all over."

"Will you hold my hand?"

Jude smiled. "Sure, baby."

A shadow stepped out of the shadows. "Young man— it's me, Lester Tinburley. I helped you fix things downstairs if you remember."

"Sure, dad, but right now I'm busy."

"I only wanted to warn you that there's another man here—" Lester's voice diminished to a dry, inaudible whisper. "I think he's going to—" He wet his lips. "—to make some sort of trouble."

Lester pointed to the crack of light under Archold's door. "Maybe you'd better get him out of the building."

"Jude—not now!"

"I'll only be a minute, baby. This could be fun." Jude looked at Lester. "Some sort of nut, huh?"

Lester nodded and retreated back into the shadow of the reception desk.

Jude pushed open the door and looked at the man who sat behind the dusty, glass-topped desk. He was old— maybe fifty—and bleary-eyed from drinking. A pushover. Jude smiled, as the man rose unsteadily to his feet.

"Get out of here!" the old man bellowed. "This is my bank. I won't have a bunch of tramps walking about in my bank."

"Hey, Jessy!" Jude called. "C'mere and getta look of this."

"Leave this room immediately. I am the president of this bank. I . . . "

Jessy giggled. "Is he crazy, or what?"

"Jack," Jude shouted into the dark reception room, "is this guy on the level? About being bank president?"

"Yessir," Lester replied.

"Lester! Are you out there? Throw these juvenile delinquents out of my bank. This minute! Do you understand? Lester!"

"Didja hear the man, Lester? Why don't you answer the bank president?"

"He can open the vault doors. You can make him do it." Lester came to stand in the door and looked in triumph at Archold. "That's where all the money is—from the other banks too. He knows the combination. There's millions of dollars. He would never do it for me, but you can make him."

"Oh Jude—let's. It would be fun. I haven't seen money for just an age."

"We don't have the time, baby."

"So we'd die at two o'clock instead of twelve. What difference would it make? Just think—a bank vault crammed full of money! Please . . . "

Archold had retreated to the corner of his office. "You can't make me ... I won't ..."

Jude began to seem more interested. He had no interest in money as such, but a contest of wills appealed to his forthright nature. "Yeah, we could toss it around like confetti—that would be something. Or build a bonfire!"

"No!" Lester gasped, then palliatively—"I'll show you where the vault is, but a fire would burn down the bank. What would the people do tomorrow night? The vault is downstairs. I've got the keys for the cage around the vault, but he'll tell you the combination."

"Lester! No!"

"Call me 'boy' like you used to, Mr. Archold. Tell me what I've got to do."

Archold grasped at the straw. "Get those two out of here. Right now, Lester."

Lester laughed. He went up to Archold's Reprostat and pressed the cigar Archtype button. He gave Jude the burning cigar. "This will make him tell you the combination." But Jude ignored Lester's advice, or seemed to. He threw away his cigarette and stuck Archold's cigar into the corner of his mouth, slightly discomposing his studied grin. Emboldened, Lester took a cigar for himself and followed this up with Scotches for himself, Jessy, and Jude. Jude sipped at his meditatively, examining Archold. When he had finished, he grabbed the bank president by the collar of his jacket and led him down the stairs to the ballroom-banking-floor.

The dancers, most of whom were shortly to die like Jude and Jessy, were desperately, giddily gay. A sixteen-year-old girl lay unconscious at the foot of the bandstand. Jude dragged Archold up the steps and into the hazy blue light. Archold noticed that Mrs. Desmond's name placard still hung on the grille of the teller's window which now formed a balustrade for the bandstand.

Jude grabbed the mike. "Stop the action. The entertainment committee has something new for all of us." The band stopped, dancers turned to look at Jude and Archold. "Ladies and gentlemen, I'd like to introduce the president of this fine bank, Mr.—what-did-you-say-your-name-was?"

"Archold," Lester volunteered from the dance floor. "Charlie Archold."

"Mr. Archold is going to open up the bank vault special for tonight's little party, and we're going to decorate the walls with good, old-fashioned dollar bills. We're going to roll in money—isn't that so, Charlie?"

Archold struggled to get loose from Jude's grip. The crowd began to laugh. "You'll pay for the damge you've done here," he moaned into the mike. "There are still laws for your kind. You can't . . ."

"Hey, Jude," a girl yelled, "lemme dance with the old fellow. You only live once and I'm going to try everything." The laughter swelled. Archold could not make out any faces in the crowd below. The laughter seemed to issue from the walls and the floor, disembodied and unreal. The band began a slow, mocking fox-trot. Archold felt himself gripped by a new set of hands. Jude let go of his collar.

"Move your feet, stupid. You can't dance standing still."

"Turn on the dizzy lights," Jessy shouted.

"You're forgetting the vaults," Lester whined at her. She took the old janitor in hand and led him up to the bandstand, where they watched Archold floundering in the arms of his tormentor.

The blue spotlight blanked out. The bank was suddenly filled with a swarm of bright red flashes, like the revolving lights mounted on police cars. That, in fact, had been their source. Klaxons sounded—someone had triggered the bank's own alarm system. A trumpet, then the drums, took up the klaxon's theme.

"Let me lead," the girl was shouting in Archold's ear. He saw her face in a brief flash of red light, cruel and avid, strangely reminiscent of Nora—but Nora was his wife and loved him—then felt himself being pushed back, his knees crumbling, over the grille and down. The girl lying on the floor broke his fall.

There were gunshots. The police, he thought. Of course there were no police. The boys were aiming at the spinning lights.

Archold felt himself lifted by dozens of hands. Lights spun around him overhead, and there was a brief explosion when one of the marksmen made a bull's-eye. The hands that bore him aloft began to pull in different directions, revolving him, cartwheeled-fashion, in time to the klaxon's deafening music, faster and faster. He felt the back of his jacket begin to rip, then a wrenching pain in his shoulder. Another explosion of light.

He fell to the floor with a shuddering pain through his whole body. He was drenched with water, lying at the door of the vault.

"Open it, dad," someone—not Jude—said.

Archold saw Lester in the forefront of the group. He raised his arm to strike at him, but the pain stopped him. He stood up and looked at the ring of adolescent faces around him. "I won't open it. That money does not belong to me. I'm responsible to the people who left it here; it's their money. I can't . . ."

"Man, nobody is going to use that money, any more. Open it."

A girl stepped out from the crowd and crossed over to Archold. She wiped his forehead where it was bleeding. "You better do what they say," she said gently. "Almost all of them are going to kill themselves tonight, and they don't care what they do or who they hurt. Life is cheap—a couple bars of carbon and a few quarts of water—and the pieces of paper behind that door don't mean a thing. In one day you could Reprostat a million dollars."

"No. I can't. I won't do it."

"Everybody—you too, Darline—get back here. We'll make him open it up." The main body of the crowd had already retreated behind the cage that fenced in the vault. Lester, of course, had had the keys to get them into the cage. Darline shrugged and joined the rest of them.

"Now, Mr. President, either you open that door or we'll start using you for a target."

"No!" Archold rushed to the combination lock. "I'll do it," he was screaming when one of the boys shot the glass-faced regulator above the lock.

"You hit him."

"I did not."

Darline went to look. "It was a heart attack, I guess. He's dead."

They left Lester alone in the outer room of the vault with Archold's body. He stared bleakly at the corpse. "I'll do it again," he said. "Again and again."

On the floor above them, the klaxons were quietened and the music began again, sweetly at first, then faster, and louder It was nearing midnight.

Nora Archold. wife of Charles, was embarrassed by her red hair. Although it was her natural color, she suspected that people thought she dyed it. She was forty-two, after all, and so many older women decided to be redheads.

"I like it just the way it is, honey," Dewey told her. "You're being silly."

"Oh, Dewey, I'm so worried."

"There isn't anything to worry about. It's not as though you were leaving him—you know that."

"But it seems *wrong*."

Dewey laughed. Nora pouted, knowing that she looked becoming in a pout. He tried to kiss her, but she pushed him away and went on with her packing—one of a kind of everything she liked. The suitcase was more of a ceremonial gesture than a practical necessity; in one afternoon at the stores she could have an entire wardrobe Reprostated if she wanted to take the trouble (a kind of trouble she enjoyed taking). But she liked her old clothes— many of which were "originals." The difference between an original and a Reprostated copy was undetectable even under an electron microscope, but Nora, none the less, felt a vague mistrust of the copies—as though they were somehow transparent to other eyes and shabbier.

"We were married twenty years ago, Charlie and me. You must have been just a little kid when I was already a married woman." Nora shook her head at woman's frailty. "And I don't even know your last name." This time she let Dewey kiss her.

"Hurry up, now," he whispered. "The old boy will be back any minute."

"It's not fair to *her*," Nora complained. "She'll have to put up with all the horrible things I have all these years."

"Make up your mind. First you worry about him; now, it isn't fair for her. I'll tell you what—when I get home, I'll Reprostat another Galahad to rescue *her* from the old dragon."

Nora observed him suspiciously. "Is that your last name —Galahad?"

"Hurry up now," he commanded.

"I want you out of the house while I do it. I don't want you to see—the other one."

Dewey guffawed. "I'll bet not!" He carried the suitcase to the car and waited while Nora watched him from the picture window. She looked about the living room once more regretfully. It was a beautiful house in one of the best suburbs. For twenty years it had been a part of her, rather the greater part She didn't have any idea where Dewey wanted to take her. She was thrilled by her own infidelity, realizing at the same time that it made no difference. As Dewey had pointed out to her, life was cheap—a couple bars of carbon and a few quarts of water.

The clock on the wall read 12:30. She had to hurry

In the Reprostating room, she unlocked the Personal panel on the control board It was meant only for emergencies, but it could be argued that this was an emergency. It had been Charles' idea to have his own body Archtyped by the Reprostat. His heart was bad; it could give out at any time, and a personal Archtype was better than life insurance. It was, in a way, almost immortality. Nora, naturally, had been Archtyped at the same time. That had been in October, seven months after the bank had closed, but it seemed like only yesterday. It was June already. With Dewey around, she'd been able to cut down on her drinking.

Nora pressed the button reading "Nora Archold." The sign on the control panel flashed INSUFFICIENT PHOSPHORUS. Nora went to the kitchen, dug into the cupboard drawers for the right jar and deposited it in the hopper that had been set into the floor. The Reprostat whirred and clicked to a stop. Timidly, Nora opened the door of the materializer.

Nora Archold—herself—lay on the floor of the chamber in an insensible heap, in the same state that Nora (the older, unfaithful Nora) had been in when—that day in October—she had been Archtyped. The elder Nora dragged her freshly Reprostated double into the bedroom She considered leaving a note that would explain what had happened—why Nora was leaving with a stranger she had met only that afternoon. But, outside the house, Dewey was honking. Tenderly, she kissed the insensible woman who lay in her own bed and left the house where she had felt, for twenty years, a prisoner.

> *Fair youth, beneath the trees thou canst not leave*
>   *Thy song, nor even can those trees be bare*

"Afraid?"
  "No. Are you?"

"Not if you hold my hand." Jude began to embrace her again. "No, just hold my hand. We could go on like this forever, and then everything would be spoiled. We'd grow old, quarrel, stop caring for each other. I don't want that to happen. Do you think it will be the same for them as it was for us?"

"It couldn't be any different."

"It *was* beautiful," Jessy said.

"Now?" Jude asked.

"Now," she consented.

Jude helped her to sit down at the edge of the hopper, then took a seat beside her. The opening was barely big enough for their two bodies. Jessy's hand tightened around Jude's fingers: the signal. Together, they slid into the machine. There was no pain, only a cessation of consciouness. Atoms slid loose from their chemical bonds instantaneously; what had been Jude and Jessy was now only increments of elementary matter in the storage chamber of the Reprostat. From those atoms, anything could be reassembled: food, clothing, a pet canary—anything that the machine possessed an Archtype of—even another Jude and Jessy.

In the next room, Jude and Jessy slept next to each other. The sodium pentothol was beginning to wear off. Jude's arm lay across Jessy's shoulder, where the newly-disintegrated Jessy had lain it before leaving them.

Jessy stirred. Jude moved his hand.

"Do you know what day it is?" she whispered.

"Hmm?"

"It's starting," she said, "This is our last day."

"It will always be that day, honey."

She began to hum a song: Now, now, now, now—Now is forever.

For ever wilt thou love, and she be fair!

At one o'clock, the last of the revelers having departed from the bank, Lester Tinburley dragged Archbold's body to the Cadillac in the street outside. He found the ignition key in Archold's pocket. It was an hour's drive to the president's suburban home—or a little longer than it took to smoke one of the cigars from the Reprostat on the dashboard.

Lester Tinburley had come to work at the New York

Exchange Bank in 1953, immediately upon his release from the Armed Services. He had seen Charles Archold rise from the bond window to a loan consultant's desk to the accounting office on the second floor and eventually to the presidency, a rise that paralleled Lester's own ascension through the ranks to the lieutenancy of the janitorial staff. The two men, each surrounded by the symbols of his authority, had had a common interest in the preservation of order—that is to say, bureaucracy. They had been allies in conservatism. The advent of the Reprostat, however, changed all that.

The Reprostat could be programmed to reproduce from its supply of elementary particles (some sub-atomic) any given mechanical, molecular, or atomic structure; any *thing*, in short. The Reprostat could even reprostat smaller Reprostats. As soon as such a machine became available to even a few, it would inevitably become available to anyone—and when anyone possessed a Reprostat he needed very little else. The marvelous machines could not provide Charles Archold with pleasant sensations of self-justification in the performance of his work and the exercise of his authority, but only the vanishing breed of the inner-directed required such intangible pleasures. The new order of society, as evidenced in Jude and Jessy, were content to take their pleasures where they found them—in the Reprostat. They lived in an eternal present which came very close to being an earthly paradise.

Lester Tinburley could not share either attitude perfectly. While Charles Archold's way of life was only affected adversely by the new abundance (he had been able, as a bank president, to afford most of the things he really desired) and Jessy and Jude indulged themselves in Arcady, Lester was torn between the new facts of life and his old habits. He had learned, in fifty years of menial work and mean living, to take a certain pleasure and a considerable amount of pride in the very meanness of his circumstances. He preferred beer to cognac, overalls to a silk lounging robe. Affluence had come too late in his life for him to do it justice, especially an affluence so divested of the symbols with which he (like Archold) had always associated it: power, the recognition of authority, and, above all else, money. Avarice is an absurd vice in the earthly paradise, but Lester's mind had been formed at an earlier time when it was still possible to be a miser.

Lester parked the Cadillac in the Archolds' two-car garage and wrestled the stiff body of the bank president into the house. Through the bedroom door he could see Nora Archold sprawled on the bed, sleeping or drunk. Lester shoved Archold's old body into the hopper of the Reprostat. The Personal panel on the control board had been left unlocked. Lester opened the door of the materializer. If he had been partly responsible for Archold's death earlier that evening, this was a perfect atonement. He felt no guilt.

He laid the drugged body of the bank president on the bed beside Nora's and watched them breathing lightly. Archold would probably be a little confused in the morning, as Lester had noticed he had been in the office. But calendar time was beginning to be less and less meaningful, when one was no longer obliged to punch a time clock or meet deadlines.

"See you tomorrow," he said to his old boss. One of these days, he was convinced, Archold would open the vault *before* his heart failed him. In the meantime, he sort of enjoyed seeing his old employer dropping in at the bank every day. It was like old times.

Charles Archold liked the façade best at twilight. On June evenings like this (or was it July?), the sun would sink into the canyon of Mawwell Street and spotlight the sculptured group in the pediment: a full-breasted Commerce extended an allegorical cornucopia from which tumbled allegorical fruits into the outstretched hands of Industry, Labor, Transportation, Science, and Art. He was idling past (the Cadillac engine was definitely getting worse), abstractedly considering the burning tip of his cigar, when he observed peripherally that Commerce had been beheaded. He stopped.

The Contest

"No."

"You didn't let me finish."

"It's still *no*."

"But I don't want money ... I just wanted to talk."

"Talk to yourself."

"I can walk as fast as you. Unless you call a policeman ..."

"If you're hustling, if you're selling something, even if you want a cigarette—No."

"Let's pretend I'm human."

"We would have nothing in common."

"Consider me a curiosity then: a part of the street, a mobile artifact. Already, you see, I have adopted your style. People passing will suppose we are discussing a matter of commerce, military secrets, commonplaces."

They walked together before the Racquet Club and were mirrored in the glass façade of the Seagram Building. Beneath their feet, sewers flowed silently into the sea.

By a curious chance, the two men wore identical suits. From the upper stories of the Pan Am Building, they were scarcely visible: all suits seemed identical from those heights.

The younger, less garrulous man stepped on a dog turd and grimaced. His companion smiled. "To pursue the metaphor," he said *apropos* this new unpleasantness, as though it had been a parenthesis in his conversation, "some poet—Goethe, I think—said that architecture is frozen ordure."

"Architecture is the empty spaces in between."

They stopped and considered these empty spaces. Light, sound, electromagnetic waves, and orgone energy contested for their attention. Somewhere, a defective toaster sent out signals to airplanes. Every five minutes a retarded child was born, but elsewhere cybernetic machines were being assembled at a much faster rate.

The elder man continued. "We could tell anecdotes. Play games. Join contests. If you still worry about money— look: fifty, sixty, seventy dollars, and these are credit cards. Which means that I've won the first contest, eh?"

"I hadn't joined."

"You want us to have nothing in common, but there is in each of us a certain residue of Christianity. We have read Dostoyevsky. We can, if we wish, feel exquisitely guilty over a number of things we have not done. We disapprove of genocide and, perhaps, bomb testing."

"That should be enough of a sop for the residue. But I concede: you may tell me an anecdote. On one condition: if at any time you falter, you have lost. You go away."

"When your turn comes, the stipulation holds."

"Begin then."

"Once I knew a girl. She's dead now, killed herself. Not on my account, of course, although we were in love. No, no—suspend your judgment a while yet; this *is* an anecdote.

"It was in the early fifties. You wouldn't remember them too well. I was the superintendent of an apartment house on East End Avenue. My responsibilities were few, and most of them I had sub-let, as it were, to my staff of doormen, janitors, and cleaning ladies. I hadn't enjoyed such leisure since leaving the Army.

"I met her at Union Square. In those days, the ghosts of old radicals had not yet deserted their soapboxes—"

"A banality. Watch yourself."

"Old men, strident, defeated, observed, like lobsters in a restaurant window, without fear of personal guilt, sometimes even with a distant compassion—although that is not necessary. A pretty metaphor, the lobsters?"

"Continue."

"For my own part, I pay no attention to politics, but even the unaffiliated can feel the presence or absence of those tensions. No, I don't mean the bomb. It's only your generation that observes everything through a gun-turret."

At 46th Street, they turned toward the East River. Tourists' cameras blinked at the vastness of the city; *12.05 exactly* displaced *12.04 and 50 seconds*. The toaster ejected two crisped pieces of rye bread, kept fresh by minute traces of formaldehyde. Steam arose mysteriously from the perforations in manhole covers. The elder man picked a ball of lint from the shoulder of his companion's suit.

"She was listening to one of those vanished ghosts, unable to lose herself in the sparse crowd."

"The lonely crowd?" his companion asked mockingly.

"The sparseness of the crowd allowed us to see each other. She half-raised her hand as though to greet me—no, as though she were identifying herself by a secret sign, a gesture of complicity. Then, she reconsidered. She must have wondered if, instead of a fellow-agent, I were an *agent-provocateur*."

"A Communist!"

"Nothing so gross. *She* was unaffiliated, I am sure. But she was in advance of history. She was terrified of the FBI, of French spies, of traffic cops, of sailors, of the Mafia, of simply everyone."

"But why?"

"She was impressionable. I introduced myself. She suspected my motives, but then all motives—the very idea of a motive—aroused her suspicions. She consented, at least, to have lunch with me."

"And, then, an affair of the heart?"

"Such as it was."

"Perhaps she needed to compromise herself."

"When she visited my rooms (for she never allowed me into hers) it was only after taking the most devious precautions. She was followed everywhere, so she claimed. She whispered—so that her voice would not be taped. She was afraid to sleep, for fear I would, perhaps, rifle her purse or notify the confederates. She admitted all this freely, and yet I don't believe she ever trusted me, even then. She always believed that I was leading her on to betray something."

"What?"

"That she would never reveal. She committed suicide before she could tell me. The curious thing happened long afterward. An FBI man came to question me about her. I assume he was from the FBI, but he might equally well have been a spy posing as a G-man. I would not have known the difference."

"And what did you tell him?"

"All that I knew, although I doubt it helped him. He seemed old enough to be her father."

"Perhaps he was."

"I didn't overlook that possibility. I didn't refer to the intimacies of our *liaison*. I pretended to friendship, but I did not confess passion."

"Your story undoubtedly has a moral."

"That what allows love still to exist in our society is precisely its totalitarianism. We made our vows under the threat of torture."

"I'm surprised she didn't prefer a lobotomy to suicide."

"Ah, she was afraid of doctors, too."

All along the street, the store-fronts defied the designs of architects made manifest in upper stories. Everywhere one looked, there were infinite, unknowable, ramifications; nexuses, relationships, tangents. One had no choice but to ignore them.

The younger man stopped to look in a shop window.

"Now it is your turn."

"I've heard all I need to," said the younger man, who was, of course, a secret agent. As a token of his love, he shot M—twice through the heart, through, that is to say, the left side of the chest. The two shots seemed to be in code.

The Empty Room

Gray slices of plaster curled down from the low ceiling. Thadeus laid his hand on Diane's woolly hip. "Do you like it?" he asked. Her hip shrugged.

The linoleum represented a large basket weave. The warp and the woof were of two colors of tan—straw and mustard. A yellow sink drooped from the wall.

"I don't think we'll do much better than this," he said.

"No," she said, uncertainly. She twisted away from him and walked to the open window. Smiling, he watched her and pretended that she was smoking a cigarette. Her exquisite hair, blond as lemonpulp, stirred in the delicate breezes.

Within the wall, mortar crumbled, and fell with a rattling sound. "We'll keep a look-out for a better place, of course," he said.

She was twenty-seven years old, or twenty-six. Except for a single summer working in New Jersey, Diane had lived all her life in New York. "We'll buy chairs," she said. "And Nathan can give us the convertible sofa he promised us last week."

He nodded eagerly.

"And you can have another set of keys made," she went on, listlessly.

"For you," Thadeus said.

"My set of keys," she said. "It will seem very real then."

"It's only temporary," he assured her again. A lie, of course—both told more for his own sake than for hers. At forty-eight, unskilled, he wasn't apt to find a better job than he had now.

Thadeus rented his brain, on a temporary basis, to small companies that couldn't afford full-time cybernation. He was, by analogy, a vacuum tube.

The Empty Room

Diane drew a face in the grime on the window.

"Who is that?" he asked.

"You," she said. "Or me."

Thadeus opened the door of the small toilet. The enamel base was capped with a black plastic cover. "Somehow," he said, reflectively, "I always expected something more . . . of life."

"Yes, I thought it would be more fun," Diane said. She took off her coat, rolled it up, laid it on the linoleum. Then sitting on the rolled coat, she began to remove her shoes.

A song floated in the open window, like smoke. Thadeus swore and slammed the window to.

"More meaningful," Diane went on.

"Is it *our fault?*" Thadeus said.

"No," said Diane. Then after a while, "I don't think so." She took off her furry stockings. Her bare legs were red with goosebumps. He imagined her lying in bed, a single, long white leg sticking out from the black sheets. He helped her unzip the back of her dress.

"Do you really love me?" she said.

"Oh yes," he said.

She stood up and he helped her pull the dress over her head. "How do you *know?*" she said.

"I fell in love with you the very first time I saw you." She nodded. She took off the paper brassière and pantilettes and handed them to him. He flushed them down the toilet. She took a new set out of her purse. She said, "I'm not sure that I love you."

"That's all right," Thadeus said. "As long as you're with me."

"Are you afraid to be alone?" she asked.

"No," he said.

She wriggled back into the dress. "I wish I could afford some nice new clothes."

"You look very nice in that dress," he said.

"Thank you," she said.

One of the larger pieces of plaster fell from the ceiling into the sink, exposing a patch of lath and wire. Thadeus swore. Diane said, "We'd better ask the landlord to do something about the ceiling before we move in."

Thadeus nodded, knowing already, however, that it was a hopeless task.

Diane sat back down on the rolled-up coat and pulled

on the stockings of synthetic white fur. "It must be a very old building."

"Listen," he said. "The water still hasn't stopped."

"Jiggle it," she said.

He went into the tiny bathroom and jiggled the chain. The water stopped. Diane had left the black plastic lid up, and he looked into the clear water of the toilet bowl. He imagined a very tiny person (in his fantasy he did not differentiate between male and female) swimming in the tiny pool of water. Then he imagined how, when the toilet was flushed, the tiny person would be sucked down into the pipes. He tried to imagine what would happen next, but couldn't.

"I'm ready," Diane said.

When he came out she was already back in her tweed-type coat. He kissed her. "Do you love me?" she asked, glancing at him sideways.

"Oh yes," he said. Then he said, "Well?"

She said, "Well, what?"

"Shall we take this place or go on looking?"

"Let's take this place," she said. "I like it."

"It's only temporary," he said. "And once it has a fresh coat of paint, it will be a lot . . . nicer."

"Do you have a pill?" she said.

He gave her one of the yellow pills. She shuddered.

"You know," he said, walking to the door across the straw and mustard floor, stepping only on the interstices of the basket, never on the warp or on the woof, ". . . maybe I am."

"Maybe you are what?" she asked, still shivering in her wooly coat.

"Maybe I am afraid of being alone."

"Of course," she said.

When they had left the room, the room was empty.

The Squirrel Cage

The terrifying thing—if that's what I mean—I'm not sure that "terrifying" is the right word—is that I'm free to write down anything I like but that no matter what I *do* write down it will make no difference—to me, to you, to whomever differences are made. But then what is meant by "a difference"? Is there ever really such a thing as change?

I ask more questions these days than formerly; I am less programmatic altogether. I wonder—is that a good thing?

This is what it is like where I am: a chair with no back to it (so I suppose you would call it a stool); a floor, walls, and a ceiling, which form, as nearly as I can judge, a cube; white, white light, no shadows—not even on the underside of the lid of the stool; me, of course; the typewriter. I have described the typewriter at length elsewhere. Perhaps I shall describe it again. Yes, almost certainly I shall. But not now. Later. Though why not now? Why not the typewriter as well as anything else?

Of the many kinds of question at my disposal, "why" seems to be the most recurrent.

What I do is this: I stand up and walk around the room from wall to wall. It is not a large room, but it's large enough for present purposes. Sometimes I even jump, but there is little incentive to do that, since there is nothing to jump *for*. The ceiling is quite too high to touch, and the stool is so low that it provides no challenge at all. If I thought anyone were *entertained* by my jumping . . . but I have no reason to suppose that. Sometimes I exercise: push-ups, somersaults, head-stands, isometrics, etc. But never as much as I should. I am getting fat. Disgustingly fat and full of pimples besides. I like to squeeze the pimples on my face. Every so often I will keep one sore

and open with overmuch pinching, in the hope that I will
develop an abscess and blood poisoning. But apparently
the place is germproof. The thing never infects.

It's well nigh impossible to kill oneself here. The walls
and floor are padded, and one only gets a headache
beating one's head against them. The stool and the
typewriter both have hard edges, but whenever I have
tried to use *them,* they're withdrawn into the floor. That is
how I know there is someone watching.

Once I was convinced it was God. I assumed that this
was either heaven or hell, and I imagined that it would go
on for all eternity just the same way. But if I were living
in eternity already, I couldn't get fatter all the time.
Nothing changes in eternity. So I console myself that I
will someday die. Man is mortal. I eat all I can to make
that day come faster. The *Times* says that that will give
me heart disease.

Eating is fun, and that's the real reason I do a lot of
eating. What else is there to do, after all? There is this
little . . . nozzle, I suppose you'd call it, that sticks out of
one wall, and all I have to do is put my mouth to it. Not
the most elegant way to feed, but it tastes damn good.
Sometimes I just stand there for hours at a time and let it
trickle in. Until *I* have to trickle. That's what the stool is
for. It has a lid on it, the stool does, which moves on a
hinge. It's quite clever, in a mechanical way.

If I sleep, I don't seem to be aware of it. Sometimes I
do catch myself dreaming, but I can never remember
what they were about. I'm not able to make myself dream
at will. I would like that exceedingly. That covers all the
vital functions but one—and there is an accommodation
for sex too. Everything has been thought of.

I have no memory of any time before this, and I cannot
say how long *this* has been going on. According to today's
New York *Times* it is the Second of May, 1961. I don't
know what conclusion one is to draw from that.

From what I've been able to gather, reading the *Times,*
my position here in this room is not typical. Prisons, for
instance seem to be run along more liberal lines, usually.
But perhaps the *Times* is lying, covering up. Perhaps even
the date has been falsified. Perhaps the entire paper, every
day, is an elaborate forgery and this is actually 1950, not
1961. Or maybe they are antiques and I am living whole

centuries after they were printed, a fossil. Anything seems possible. I have no way to judge.

Sometimes I make up little stories while I sit here on my stool in front of the typewriter. Sometimes they are stories about the people in the New York *Times*, and those are the best stories. Sometimes they are just about people I make up, but those aren't so good because . . .

They're not so good because I think everybody is dead. I think I may be the only one left, sole survivor of the breed. And they just keep me here, the last one, alive, in this room, this cage, to look at, to observe, to make their observations of, to—I don't *know* why they keep me alive. And if everyone is dead, as I've supposed, then who are they, these supposed observers? Aliens? *Are* there aliens? I don't know. Why are they studying me? What do they hope to learn? Is it an experiment? What am I supposed to do? Are they waiting for me to say something, to write something on this typewriter? Do my responses or lack of responses confirm or destroy a theory of behavior? Are the testers happy with their results? They give no indications. They efface themselves, veiling themselves behind these walls, this ceiling, this floor. Perhaps no human could stand the sight of them. But maybe they are only scientists, and not aliens at all. Psychologists at MIT perhaps, such as frequently are shown in the *Times*: blurred, dotty faces, bald heads, occasionally a mustache, certificate of originality. Or, instead, young crewcut Army doctors studying various brainwashing techniques. Reluctantly, of course. History and a concern for freedom has forced them to violate their own (privately held) moral codes. Maybe I *volunteered* for this experiment! Is that the case? O God, I hope not! Are you reading this, Professor? Are you reading this, Major? Will you let me out now? I want to leave this experiment *right now*.

Yeah.

Well, we've been through that little song and dance before, me and my typewriter. We've tried just about every password there is. Haven't we, typewriter? And as you can see (can you see?)—here we are still.

They are aliens, obviously.

Sometimes I write poems. Do you like poetry? Here's one of the poems I wrote. It's called *Grand Central Terminal*. ("Grand Central Terminal" is the right name for what

most people wrongly call "Grand Central Station." This—
and other priceless information—comes from the New
York *Times*.).

> *Grand Central Terminal*
>
> How can you be unhappy
> when you see how high
> the ceiling is?
>
>   My!
>
> the ceiling is high!
> High as the sky!
> So who are *we*
> to be gloomy here?
>
>   Why,
>
> there isn't even room
> to die, my dear.
>
> This is the tomb
> of some giant so great
> that if he ate
> us there would be
> simply no taste.
>
>   Gee,
>
> what a waste
> that would be
> of you and me.

And sometimes, as you can also see, I just sit here
copying old poems over again, or maybe copying the
poem that the *Times* prints each day. The *Times* is my
only source of poetry. Alas the day! I wrote *Grand Central Terminal* rather a long time ago. Years. I can't say
exactly how many years though.

I have no measures of time here. No day, no night, no
waking and sleeping, no chronometer but the *Times*, ticking off its dates. I can remember dates as far back as
1957. I wish I had a little diary that I could keep here in
the room with me. Some record of my progress. If I could
just save up my old copies of the *Times*. Imagine how,
over the years, they would pile up. Towers and stairways

and cozy burrows of newsprint. It would be a more humane architecture, would it not? This cube that I occupy does have drawbacks from the strictly human point of view. But I am not allowed to keep yesterday's edition. It is always taken away, whisked off, before today's edition is delivered. I should be thankful, I suppose, for what I have.

What if the *Times* went bankrupt? What if, as is often threatened, there were a newspaper strike! Boredom is not, as you might suppose, the great problem. Eventually—very soon, in fact—boredom becomes a great challenge. A stimulus.

My body. Would you be interested in my body? I used to be. I used to regret that there were no mirrors in here. Now, on the contrary, I am grateful. How gracefully, in those early days, the flesh would wrap itself about the skeleton; now, how it droops and languishes! I used to dance by myself hours on end, humming my own accompaniment—leaping, rolling about, hurling myself spread-eagled against the padded walls. I became a connoisseur of kinethesia. There is great joy in movement—free, unconstrained speed.

Life is so much tamer now. Age dulls the edge of pleasure, hanging in wreathes of fat on the supple Christmas tree of youth.

I have various theories about the meaning of life. Of life *here*. If I were somewhere else—in the world I know of from the New York *Times,* for instance, where so many exciting things happen every *day* that it takes half a million words to tell about them—there would be no problem at all. One would be so busy running around—from 53rd Street to 42nd Street from 42nd Street to the Fulton Street Fish Market, not to mention all the journeys one might make *crosstown*—that one wouldn't have to worry whether life had a meaning.

In the daytime one could shop for a multitude of goods, then in the evening, after a dinner at a fine restaurant, to the theater or a cinema. Oh, life would be so full if I were living in New York! If I were free! I spend a lot of time, like this, imagining what New York must be like, imagining what other people are like, what I would be like with other people, and in a sense my life here is full from imagining such things.

One of my theories is that they (*you* know, ungentle

reader, who they are, I'm sure) are waiting for me to make a confession. This poses problems. Since I remember nothing of my previous existence, I don't know what I should confess. I've tried confessing to everything: political crimes, sex crimes (I especially like to confess to sex crimes), traffic offenses, spiritual pride. My god, what *haven't* I confessed to? Nothing seems to work. Perhaps I just haven't confessed to the crimes I really did commit, whatever they were. Or perhaps (which seems more and more likely) the theory is at fault.

I have another theory.

A brief hiatus.

The *Times* came, so I read the day's news, then nourished myself at the fount of life, and now I am back at my stool.

I have been wondering whether, if I were living in that world, the world of the *Times*, I would be a pacifist or not. It is certainly the central issue of modern morality and one would have to take a stand. I have been thinking about the problem for some years, and I am inclined to believe that I am in favor of disarmament. On the other hand, in a practical sense I wouldn't object to the bomb if I could be sure it would be dropped on me. There is definitely a schism in my being between the private sphere and the public sphere.

On one of the inner pages, behind the political and international news, was a wonderful story headlined: BIOLOGISTS HAIL MAJOR DISCOVERY. Let me copy it out for your benefit:

Washington D.C.—Deep-sea creatures with brains but no mouths are being hailed as a major biological discovery of the twentieth century.

The weird animals, known as pogonophores, resemble slender worms. Unlike ordinary worms, however, they have no digestive system, no excretory organs, and no means of breathing, the National Geographic Society says. Baffled scientists who first examined pogonophores believed that only parts of the specimens had reached them.

Biologists are now confident that they have seen the whole animal, but still do not understand how it manages to live. Yet they know it does exist, propagate, and even think, after a fashion, on the floors of deep waters around the globe. The female pogonophore lays up to thirty eggs at a time. A tiny brain permits rudimentary mental processes.

All told, the pogonophore is so unusual that biologists have set up a special phylum for it alone. This is significant because a phylum is such a broad biological classification that creatures as diverse as fish, reptiles, birds, and men are all included in the phylum Chordata.

Settling on the sea bottom, a pogonophore secretes a tube around itself and builds it up, year by year, to a height of perhaps five feet. The tube resembles a leaf of white grass, which may account for the fact that the animal went so long undiscovered.

The pogonophore apparently never leaves its self-built prison, but crawls up and down inside at will. The wormlike animal may reach a length of fourteen inches, with a diameter of less than a twenty-fifth of an inch. Long tentacles wave from its top end.

Zoologists once theorized that the pogonophore, in an early stage, might store enough food in its body to allow it to fast later on. But young pogonophores also lack a digestive system.

It's amazing the amount of things a person can learn just by reading the *Times* every day. I always feel so much more *alert* after a good read at the paper. And creative. Herewith, a story about pogonophores:

STRIVING

The Memoirs of a Pogonophore

Introduction

In May of 1961 I had been considering the purchase of a pet. One of my friends had recently acquired a pair of tarsiers, another had adopted a boa constrictor, and my nocturnal roommate kept an owl caged above his desk.

A nest (or school?) of pogs was certainly one-up on their eccentricities. Moreover, since pogonophores do not eat, excrete, sleep, or make noise, they would be ideal pets. In June I had three dozen shipped to me from Japan at considerable expense.

[A brief interruption in the story: Do you feel that it's credible? Does it possess the *texture* of reality? I thought that by beginning the story by mentioning those other pets, I would clothe my invention in greater verisimilitude. Were you taken in?]

Being but an indifferent biologist, I had not considered the problem of maintaining adequate pressure in my aquarium. The pogonophore is used to the weight of an entire ocean. I was not equipped to meet such demands. For a few exciting days I watched the surviving pogs rise and descend in their translucent white shells. Soon, even these died. Now, resigned to the commonplace, I stock my aquarium with Maine lobsters for the amusement and dinners of occasional out-of-town visitors.

I have never regretted the money I spent on them: man is rarely given to know the sublime spectacle of the rising pogonophore—and then but briefly. Although I had at that time only the narrowest conception of the thoughts that passed through the rudimentary brain of the sea worm ("Up up up Down down down"), I could not help admiring its persistence. The pogonophore does not sleep. He climbs to the top of the inside passage of his shell, and, when he has reached the top, he retraces his steps to the bottom of his shell. The pogonophore never tires of his self-imposed regimen. He performs his duty scrupulously and with honest joy. He is *not* a fatalist.

The memoirs that follow this introduction are not allegory. I have not tried to "interpret" the inner thoughts of the pogonophore. There is no need for that, since the pogonophore himself has given us the most eloquent record of his spiritual life. It is transcribed on the core of translucent white shell in which he spends his entire life.

Since the invention of the alphabet it has been a common conceit that the markings on shells or the sand-etched calligraphy of the journeying snail are possessed of true linguistic meaning. Cranks and eccentrics down the ages have tried to decipher these codes, just as other men have sought to understand the language of the birds. Unavailingly. I do not claim that the scrawls and shells of *common* shellfish can be translated; the core of the pogonophore's shell, however can be—for I have broken the code!

With the aid of a United States Army manual on cryptography (obtained by what devious means I am not at liberty to reveal) I have learned the grammar and syntax of the pogonophore's secret language. Zoologists and others who would like to verify my solution of the crypt may reach me through the editor of this publication.

In all thirty-six cases I have been able to examine, the indented traceries on the insides of these shells have been the same. It is my theory that the sole purpose of the pogonophore's tentacles is to follow the course of this "message" up and down the core of his shell and thus, as it were, to think. The shell is a sort of externalized stream-of-consciousness.

It would be possible (and in fact it is an almost irresistible temptation) to comment on the meaning that these memoirs possess for mankind. Surely, there is a philosophy compressed into these precious shells by Nature herself. But before I begin my commentary, let us examine the text itself.

The Text

I
Up. Uppity, up, up. The top.
II
Down. Downy, down, down. Thump. The Bottom.
III

A description of my typewriter. The keyboard is about one foot wide. Each key is flush to the next and marked with a single letter of the alphabet, or with two punctuation signs, or with one number and one punctuation sign. The letters are not ordered as they are in the alphabet, alphabetically, but seemingly at random. It is possible that they are in code. Then there is a space bar. There is not, however, either a margin control or a carriage return. The platen is not visible, and I can never see the words I'm writing. What does it all look like? Perhaps it is made immediately into a book by automatic linotypists. Wouldn't that be nice? Or perhaps my words just go on and on in one endless line of writing. Or perhaps this typewriter is just a fraud and leaves no record at all.

Some thoughts on the subject of futility:

I might just as well be lifting weights as pounding at these keys. Or rolling stones up to the top of a hill from which they immediately roll back down. Yes, and I might as well tell lies as the truth. It makes no difference what I say.

That is what is so terrifying. Is "terrifying" the right word?

I seem to be feeling rather poorly today, but I've felt poorly before! In a few more days I'll be feeling all right again. I need only be patient, and then ...

What do they want of me here? If only I could be sure that I were serving some good *purpose*. I cannot help worrying about such things. Time is running out. I'm hungry again. I suspect I am going crazy. That is the end of my story about the pogonophores.

A hiatus.

Don't *you* worry that I'm going crazy? What if I got catatonia? Then *you'd* have nothing to read. Unless they gave *you* my copies of the New York Times. It would serve *you* right.

You: the mirror that is denied to me, the shadow that I do not cast, my faithful observer, who reads each freshly-minted *pensée;* Reader.

You: Horrorshow monster, Bug-Eyes, Mad Scientist, Army Major, who prepares the wedding bed of my death and tempts me to it.

You: Other!
Speak to me!

YOU: What shall I say, Earthling?

I: Anything so long as it is another voice than my own, flesh that is not my own flesh, lies that I do not need to invent for myself. I'm not particular, I'm not proud. But I doubt sometimes—you won't think this is too melodramatic of me?—that I'm real.

YOU: I know the feeling. (Extending a tentacle) May I?

I: (Backing off) Later. Just now I thought we'd talk. (You begin to fade.)
There is so much about you that I don't understand. Your identity is not distinct. You change from one being to another as easily as I might switch channels on a television set, if I had one.

> You are too secretive as well. You should get about in the world more. Go places, show yourself, enjoy life. If you're shy, I'll go out with you. You let yourself be undermined by fear, however.

YOU: Interesting. Yes, definitely most interesting. The subject evidences acute paranoid tendencies, fantasies with almost delusional intensity. Observe his tongue, his pulse, his urine. His stools are irregular. His teeth are bad. He is losing his hair.

I: I'm losing my mind.

YOU: He's losing his mind.

I: I'm dying.

YOU: He's dead.
(Fades until there is nothing but the golden glow of the eagle on his cap, a glint from the oak leaves on his shoulders.) But he has not died in vain. His country will always remember him, for by his death he has made this nation free.

(Curtain. Anthem.)

Hi, it's me again. Surely you haven't forgotten *me?* Your old friend, me? Listen carefully now—this is my plan. I'm going to escape from this damned prison, by God, and *you're* going to help me. 20 people may read what I write on this typewriter, and of those 20, 19 could see me rot here forever without batting an eyelash. But not number 20. Oh no! He—*you*—still has a conscience. He/you will send me a Sign. And when I've seen the Sign, I'll know that someone out there is trying to help. Oh, I won't expect miracles overnight. It may take months, years even, to work out a foolproof escape, but just the knowledge that there is someone out there trying to help will give me the strength to go on from day to day, from issue to issue of the *Times*.

You know what I sometimes wonder? I sometimes wonder why the *Times* doesn't have an editorial about me. They state their opinion on everything else—Castro's

Cuba, the shame of our southern states, the sales tax, the first days of spring.

What about me!

I mean, isn't it an injustice the way *I'm* being treated? Doesn't anybody care and if not, why not? Don't tell me they don't know I'm here. I've been years now writing, writing. Surely they have some idea. Surely *someone* does!

These are serious questions. They demand serious appraisal. I insist that they be *answered*.

I don't really expect an answer, you know. I have no false hopes left, none. I know there's no Sign that will be shown me, that even if there is, it will be a lie, a lure to go on hoping. I know that I am alone in my fight against this injustice. I know all that—and *I don't care!* My will is still unbroken, and my spirit free. From my isolation, out of the stillness, from the depths of this white, white light, I say this to you—I DEFY YOU! Do you hear that? I said: I DEFY YOU!

Dinner again. Where does the time all go to?

While I was eating dinner I had an idea for something I was going to say here, but I seem to have forgotten what it was. If I remember, I'll jot it down. Meanwhile, I'll tell you about my other theory.

My *other* theory is that this is a squirrel cage. You know? Like the kind you find in a small town park. You might even have one of your own, since they don't have to be very big. A squirrel cage is like most any other kind of cage except it has an exercise wheel. The squirrel gets *into* the wheel and starts running. His running makes the wheel turn, and the turning of the wheel makes it necessary for him to keep running inside it. The exercise is supposed to keep the squirrel healthy. What I don't understand is why they put the squirrel in the cage in the first place. Don't they know what it's going to be like for the poor little squirrel? Or don't they care?

They don't care.

I remember now what it was I'd forgotten. I thought of a new story. I call it "An Afternoon at the Zoo." I made it up myself. It's very short, and it has a moral. This is my story:

AN AFTERNOON AT THE ZOO

This is the story about Alexandra. Alexandra was the wife of a famous journalist, who specialized in science reporting. His work took him to all parts of the country, and since they had not been blessed with children, Alexandra often accompanied him. However this often became very boring, so she had to find something to do to pass the time. If she had seen all the movies playing in the town they were in, she might go to a museum, or perhaps to a ball game, if she were interested in seeing a ball game that day. One day she went to a zoo.

Of course it was a small zoo, because this was a small town. Tasteful but not spectacular. There was a brook that meandered all about the grounds. Ducks and a lone black swan glided among the willow branches and waddled out onto the lawn to snap up bread crumbs from the visitors. Alexandra thought the swan was beautiful.

Then she went to a wooden building called the "Rodentiary." The cages advertised rabbits, otters, raccoons, etc. Inside the cages was a litter of nibbled vegetables and droppings of various shapes and colors. The animals must have been behind the wooden partitions, sleeping. Alexandra found this disappointing, but she told herself that rodents were hardly the most important thing to see at any zoo.

Nearby the Rodentiary, a black bear was sunning himself on a rock ledge. Alexandra walked all about the demi-lune of bars without seeing other members of the bear's family. He was an enormous bear.

She watched the seals splash about in their concrete pool, and then she moved on to find the Monkey House. She asked a friendly peanut vendor where it was, and he told her it was closed for repairs.

"How sad!" Alexandra exclaimed.

"Why don't you try *Snakes and Lizards?*" the peanut vendor asked.

Alexandra wrinkled her nose in disgust. She'd hated reptiles ever since she was a little girl. Even though the Monkey House was closed she bought a bag of peanuts and ate them herself. The peanuts made her thirsty, so she bought a soft drink and sipped it through a straw, worrying about her weight all the while.

She watched peacocks and a nervous antelope, then turned off on to a path that took her into a glade of trees. Poplar trees, perhaps. She was alone there, so she took off her shoes and wiggled her toes, or performed some equivalent action. She liked to be alone like this sometimes.

A file of heavy iron bars beyond the glade of trees drew Alexandra's attention. Inside the bars there was a man, dressed in a loose-fitting cotton suit—pajamas, most likely —held up about the waist with a sort of rope. He sat on the floor of his cage without looking at anything in particular. The sign at the base of the fence read:

Chordate.

"How lovely!" Alexandra exclaimed.

Actually, that's a very old story. I tell it a different way every time. Sometimes it goes on from the point where I left off. Sometimes Alexandra talks to the man behind the bars. Sometimes they fall in love, and she tries to help him escape. Sometimes they're both killed in the attempt, and that is *very* touching. Sometimes they get caught and are put behind the bars *together*. But because they love each other so much, imprisonment is easy to endure. That is also touching, in its way. Sometimes they make it to freedom. After that though, after they're free, I never know what to do with the story. However, I'm sure that if I were free myself, free of this cage, it would not be a problem.

One part of the story doesn't make much sense. Who would put a person in a zoo? Me, for instance. Who would do such a thing? Aliens? Are we back to aliens again? Who can say about aliens? I mean, *I* don't know anything about them.

My theory, my best theory, is that I'm being kept here by people. Just ordinary people. It's an ordinary zoo, and ordinary people come by to look at me through the walls. They read the things I type on this typewriter as it appears on a great illuminated billboard, like the one that spells out the news headlines around the sides of The Times Tower on 42nd Street. When I write something funny, they may laugh, and when I write something serious, such as an appeal for help, they probably get bored and stop reading. Or vice versa perhaps. In any case, they don't take what I say very seriously. None of them care that I'm inside here. To them I'm just another animal in a cage. You might object that a human being is not the same thing as an animal, but isn't he, after all? They, the spectators, seem to think so. In any case, none of them is going to help me get out. None of them thinks it's at all strange or unusual that I'm in here. None of them thinks it's wrong. That's the terrifying thing.

"Terrifying"?

It's not terrifying. How can it be? It's only a story, after all. Maybe *you* don't think it's a story, because you're out there reading it on the billboard, but I know it's a story because I have to sit here on this stool making it up. Oh, it might have been terrifying once upon a time, when I first got the idea, but I've been here now for years. Years. The story has gone on far too long. Nothing can be terrifying for years on end. I only *say* it's terrifying because, you know, I have to say something. Something or other. The only thing that could terrify me now is if someone were to come in. If they came in and said, "All right, Disch, you can go now." That, truly, would be terrifying.

The Number You Have Reached

After the boredom had gone on long enough, the panic set in. This time it came midway through Volume 6 of Toynbee. Usually a long swim would have taken care of things, but now it was winter. He went out on the veranda in his T-shirt and let the wind from the lake rasp at his exposed flesh. He looked at the city buried in snow, and the great unblemished whiteness of the scene made his heart ache with the sense of his own loss and because it was so beautiful, too. He grasped the balcony rail, and the cold metal pricked the warm skin of his palms. His muscles ached to be used. His flesh needed the touch of other flesh. His mind needed to come up against another mind. He had to talk.

He hadn't realized how hard he had been straining on the iron rail until he had torn it loose from the two pins that moored it to the cantilevered slab of the balcony. He let go of the railing and watched it drop the fourteen stories to the street into soft, powdery snow.

The next day was better. He was back under control. Of course he had had to put Toynbee away for the time being. He exercised, carrying up heavy boxes of books and canned food from the lobby. He took a mental count of the steps. From the lobby to the second floor there were eighteen steps, and fifteen between all the other floors. One hundred and ninety-eight, all told. It upset him that the total figure stopped just two short of two hundred. As soon as he had reached, panting, the last step, his mind would continue independently: one hundred and ninety-nine, two hundred.

Once all the parcels had been put away, he began to

114

clean up. As usual, he had let the apartment become very messy. He swept out all the rooms, taking the sweepings to the veranda and releasing them into the still fierce wind. Then, in old, old clothes, down on his hands and knees, he scrubbed the wooden floors, bearing down with both hands on the stiff brush, counting the strokes. Then he waxed the floorboards till they gleamed. He dusted and waxed the furniture and tried to do the windows too, but the Wind-ex froze on the cold glass. When he was very tired, he tried to read again—a mystery, no more than that—but the only thing that interested him, the thing to which his eyes forever returned, was the number on the corner of each page. The book was 160 pages, from which he subtracted the number of the page he was on in order to arrive at the amount that there was still left for him to read. At about one o'clock he laid the book down and listened to the lake wind slamming at the windows and, beneath that, the demure ticking of the eight-day clock. That night he dreamed that he was making love to his wife, who was dead.

He heard the phone ring, and for a while he only watched it, but a phone that is ringing looks just the same as a phone that is not ringing. At last he lifted the receiver and held it to his ear. "Hello!" he said, and then: "Hello?"

"Hello," she replied, very matter-of-factly.

"I didn't think the phones were working," he said. It was a silly thing to say on such an occasion, but he had avoided a sanctimonious *Thank heaven!* or the bathos of *Speak to me, say anything, but speak to me!*

"It's the automation, I guess. Lots of things are still working, if you pay your bills."

"I like your voice," he said. "I like the sound of it."

"It's a husky voice," she said.

"It reminds me of my wife."

"Was she beautiful?"

"Lidia was very beautiful. She was the Homecoming Queen at UCLA."

"What were you?"

"I went to another school."

"That doesn't answer my question."

He blushed; she was so blunt. "I was the captain of the football team. What else?" He laughed deprecatingly. "If you'd like, I'll show you my picture in the yearbook."

"Over the telephone?" This, in a very cool tone.

"Won't you come here?"

"Not yet."

"Why not?" Tears welled up into his eyes. His stomach knotted, suddenly, as though the illimitable loss of these last years were concentrated in that single reply.

"I don't know you well enough," she explained.

"How do you know me at all? How did you know to call me here? Do you know what I think? I don't even think you exist! I'm just imagining you."

"But you'll still talk to me, won't you?"

He made no reply.

"If you like," she said, "I'll talk to you. I've been watching you for a long time, actually. The day before yesterday I saw you out on your veranda. You stood there such a long time in just your T-shirt that it made *me* feel cold. Your name is Justin Holt. I saw that on your mailbox, and, of course, then I realized who you were."

"What's your name?"

"You're that astronaut. I read all about you at the library."

"Yeah, that's who I am, all right. I'll bet you haven't even bothered to think up a name for yourself. Or a background either."

"I'm not going to tell you my name. You wouldn't believe it. But I grew up in Winnetka, outside Chicago, just like your darling Lidia, and I went to college at Bennington, though I *wasn't* Homecoming Queen. I majored in Home Ec."

"You can't do that at Bennington. It's not that kind of college."

She giggled. "I'm making fun of you, Justin. Because I know Lidia studied Home Ec, at UCLA. It was in the wedding announcement in the *Tribune*. God, but a person must be dumb to do that. I can't stand dumb people. Can you, Justin?"

His hand tightened around the receiver. "How do you know—" But he broke off, realizing his dilemma: either she was real and could not have known these things about Lidia—or he was imagining her, in which case anything she said about Lidia or himself, came from his own mind.

"I can read between the lines," she said, as though sensing his doubt. "I've seen a lot of Lidias."

"And a lot of my sort, too?"

"Oh, no, Justin. You're unique. You're famous. And you're handsome. Did you know that women think you're very handsome? And you're a genius, of course. You have an IQ of 198." Her laughter had a cruel animal resonance.

"Why'd you say that?" he asked, sure that the phantasm had betrayed itself for what it was.

"Why not? One number's as good as another."

"Then dial another number," he said, and hung up. Abruptly, he had ceased believing in her. He had always feared that it would end like this, in madness. His exercises in stoicism, his restraint, all his efforts to conserve himself had come at last to nothing.

He drank, sitting cross-legged on the splendid polar bear rug in the middle of the living room. He drank Chivas Regal from the bottle and ate English water biscuits from a tin.

When he woke the phone was ringing again. There were two mice in the biscuit tin, eating crumbs. They paid no attention to the ringing of the phone, but when he got up, they scuttered away. He picked up the phone. It wasn't morning yet. Perhaps it had only just turned dark.

"Hello," she said. "This is Justine."

He laughed, and a stabbing pain tore through his head.

"I told you you wouldn't believe me, but what did you want me to do—lie? It wouldn't have been hard to invent some more probable name. Like Mary. What do you think of Mary? Or Lidia? That sounds about as common as dishwater."

"Why do you have to pick on her?"

"Maybe I'm jealous."

"Well, you don't have to be."

"You didn't really love her, did you? You married her just the way you joined the Army, just the way you got yourself picked to go to Mars. That's all you cared for— to get to Mars. And you married Lidia because her father would help you get there."

"Listen, *Justine*," he said, "this is getting tiresome. I don't need you to call and be my guilty conscience. If you're a real person, prove it. But, right now, I don't know a thing about you."

"That's not all you don't know about. What about the millions—"

"The millions?" he interrupted her.

"—of dead," she said. "All of them dead. Everyone dead. Because of you and the others like you. The football captains and the soldiers and all the other heroes."

"I didn't do it. I wasn't even here when it happened. You can't blame me."

"Well, I am blaming you, baby. Because if you'd been ordered to, you would have done it. You'd do it now—when there's just the two of us left. Because somewhere deep in your atrophied soul *you want to*."

"You'd know that territory better than me. You grew up there."

"You think I don't exist? Maybe you think the others didn't exist either? Lidia—and all the millions of others."

"It's funny you should say that."

She was ominously quiet.

He went on, intrigued by the novelty of the idea. "That's how it feels in space. It's more beautiful than anything else there is. You're alone in the ship, and even if you're not alone you can't *see* the others. You can see the dials and the millions of stars on the screen in front of you and you can hear the voices through the earphones, but that's as far as it goes. You begin to think that the others *don't* exist."

"You know what you should do?" she said.

"What?"

"Go jump in the lake."

"That isn't funny."

There was no reply. The dial tone buzzed in his ear. She had hung up on *him* this time. He went to look out the windows at the city, buried under the tons of snow that would not be removed, but the window panes were beaded with frozen droplets of Wind-ex. He picked them off with his fingernails, one by one, counting them. When he got to one hundred and ninety-eight, the rage boiled up into one vicious gesture and he slammed his fist into the pane. The cold air rushed in on him, and he made a sound deep in his throat, beyond the sound of simple pain; it was the sound of an animal at bay.

The furnace in the building was automatic. The telephone was automatic, as long as he paid his bills, and the bank that paid his bills was automatic as long as it received his paychecks and his paychecks came automatically through the mails from the Federal Government. The entire city was run by automatons, which, one by one, ran down as the fuel or the instructions or the repairs failed them. Even the bombs had been automatic. And the spaceship that had taken him and his companions to Mars and then taken him back, they had been automatic too. Sometimes *he* felt automatic, though as an astronaut he was uniquely equipped to endure his isolation, and he had up to this point kept from panicking too badly. Even in that first week, driving up from the Cape, he had not betrayed the protective mask of smooth inexpressiveness (which he had first consciously assumed in boot camp, but which, unconsciously, temperamentally, he might almost have been born with). Of course, it had helped that the automatic street cleaners had cleared away the dead bodies, and that on highways the stalled cars had been removed. At the same time he had reflected that it was strange, it was really quite remarkable that he had been a soldier, an officer in the United States Army, for twelve years and he had never seen a dead body. Naturally, he did eventually find some that hadn't been disposed of. Lidia, for instance, seemed to have been sleeping when the bombs came. She had been in bed, in any case. The body hadn't decayed, for the bombs had been thorough in eliminating life. The vermin had only begun to reappear recently, and God knew where they had come from. The body had just sort of fallen apart.

She kept trying to telephone him, but when he answered the only thing she would say was that he should kill himself since he had killed everyone else. He pointed out that he hadn't killed her, Justine. "Oh, but *I* don't exist!" It did no good to be reasonable with her, so at last he stopped answering the phone. He would sit in the living room on the sofa with a book in his lap and count the rings. Sometimes she would let it go on interminably and he would leave the house and find a bench that faced the frozen marina. He had decided to brush up on his math. He had forgotten almost everything he had learned in college. The necessity of ignoring the cold made it easier, in a way to concentrate. When he was really involved with his studies, nothing else mattered. Or, when the wind off the lake was too strong, he might walk down the snow-bound streets, past the numbered buildings, exercising his memory, for this was, after all, the city he had grown up in. He found that he could not remember many of the particulars of his boyhood days. Memories that he had thought secure, had, through neglect, diminished almost to vanishing. So that, sometimes, trudging through the snow, he would just count his footsteps. It seemed that he might, if he kept counting long enough, come up with just the right number, and it would *count* for something. But, while he waited for that number to turn up, he knew enough about math to be entertained and even instructed. Consider the number 90. 90 was the sum of two squares: the square of 9 and the square of 3. It was also the product of 9 and 10, whereas the product of 9 and 11 was 99. And twice 99 was 198! The numbers on either side of 198 were both primes: 197 and 199. The possibilities latent in number were infinite—literally infinite.

But behind this growing passion for numbers there was an unresolved anguish, a moral restlessness, a sense of betrayal—though a betrayal of whom he could not have said. One would not exactly have called it *guilt*. It was something that Justine had aroused in him. Perhaps there was a sort of justice in her demand that he should die. There was at least no reason for him to survive. He had done nothing to deserve to be thus singled out. He had been bundled into an automated rocket with two other men and been shipped, like so much cargo, to another planet where he had stayed only long enough to witness the accidental deaths of his companions, and then he had been shunted back to his starting point. It had been the merest coincidence that in the interval the buttons had been pushed that set into motion the automated engines of destruction that in their own way possessed the secret of life and death: the neutron bombs.

Sunset especially terrified him. He was not afraid of the dark, but at sunset he had to be indoors. He would go into the kitchen, where there were no windows, and close the door behind him. After sunset, he could go anywhere in the apartment.

The counting had become a compulsion for him. From the very first day he had had a sense of what it might become. He counted the books on his shelves. He counted his own pulse. He counted off seconds by his watch. He tried to keep track of the ticking of the eight-day clock in the living room. He lay awake in bed for hours before he could sleep, counting.

One night he heard a voice in his dreams singing the nursery song about the clock:

> Hickory-dickory-dock,
> The mouse ran up the clock.
> The clock struck one,
> The mouse ran down.
> Hickory-dickory-dock.

The phone rang. Before he was quite aware, he answered it. "Please," she said, "listen to me. I'm sorry for what I said. I didn't really mean it. Don't you know that? It's been my fault from the very first. You won't do that—you won't do what I said? God, I was so afraid you wouldn't answer." She rattled on incoherently. He felt as though he were at a great remove from the voice at the other end of the wire, as though he were eavesdropping or as though she had dialed his number by mistake.

"Can I come over there now? I should have done that right at the beginning, but I was afraid. I didn't know you. *Can I come over there now?*"

He didn't know what to answer. What could he say to someone who didn't exist? The bedroom, he noticed, was drenched in moonlight. It streamed in through the thin muslin curtains and lay on the bed, as tangible as buttermilk.

"What?" he said, abstractedly.

"But perhaps I should decide it by myself alone. Is that what you think? You're right. I will come. I'll be there in ... in an hour. Or, at the very most, an hour and a half." She hung up.

He looked at the clock. I have ninety minutes, he thought. Five thousand four hundred seconds. He began to count them.

It was hard to do a number a second once you were past one hundred, so when the knock came at the door, he was only at two thousand six hundred and seventy. He tried to ignore her knocking, as he had ignored the ringing of the phone for so many days.

"Please, Justin. Please let me in."

"No," he explained carefully. "If I let you in now, I can't turn back. I'll have admitted that you're real."

"I *am* real, Justin. You can feel me, you can look at me. Oh please, Justin!"

"That's just what I'm afraid of. I'll never know whether I haven't gone completely mad at last."

"Justin, I love you."

"You don't understand, do you? You can see why it's impossible?"

"I won't leave this door. I'll stay here and when you come out—"

"I won't come out, Justine. If you had only come to me at the beginning—instead of phoning. Now it's too late. How can I believe in you now? It would be despicable to relent now, a weakness. Unforgivable. I couldn't stand that, and you could never respect me."

There was no reply from behind the door.

"Go away," he said.

He knew that she was waiting there, baiting her trap with silence. He went out on to the veranda and looked at the snow-laden city. It seemed almost brighter in moonlight than under the full glare of the sun.

I'll jump when I've counted ten, he told himself. He counted to ten, but he didn't jump. If he went back to the door, he knew she'd be there—or, at least, that he would think she was there. He had no choice. And wasn't this what she had asked of him? Wasn't this, almost, justice?

He counted to twenty, to fifty, to one hundred. The numbers had a calming effect. They made sense. Each number was just one more than the number that had preceded it, and the next number was one more than that. He counted as far as one hundred and ninety-eight. Suddenly, the knocking on the door was renewed, louder than ever. He let himself go and his body dropped the fourteen stories to the street into soft, powdery snow.

I-A

"Now *that*," Mr. Green said with great definiteness, "that was a *real* war." Mr. Green, who had been a sergeant way back in the Second World War, set the lawn rake just inside the door to his garage.

"Well, this one is probably *real* enough, for that matter," Bruce Berwyn argued, without great conviction.

Mr. Green made a skeptical sound through his nose, or perhaps it was just the strain of lifting the bushel basket of dry leaves.

"Here, let me help you with that," Bruce offered. Bruce was twenty years old and worked, with his father, as a piano mover. Two years earlier he had played fullback for his high school team, where he had shown such aptitude that, had he been willing to go to college, he would have had his choice of four scholarships, one of them in the East.

"You just look after yourself, young fellow, and that'll keep you plenty busy. I guess I've still got the strength to lift a basket of leaves." He upended them into a rusty open-ended oil drum.

"Well, you've got to admit it's necessary, Mr. Green. We've got to live up to our commitments. You've got to admit that."

Mr. Green sprinkled kerosene over the leaves. "I'll admit it keeps young people off the streets," he said with a dry chuckle.

"But the Communists—" Bruce explained patiently, ignoring the old man's gibe.

"Those goddamn reds!" Mr. Green said, applying a match. "They should have bombed China years ago. We missed our big chance in '45. We could have wiped them out of existence." A geyser of bright orange flame shot up from the top of the can, and Mr. Green bit his lower lip with satisfaction. Then, returning to his earlier theme, he said, "Now *that* was a real war. Goddamned yellowbelly Japs—I could tell you stories about those babies that would make your *teeth* fall out. We should have bombed them while we had the chance."

"But they're our *allies*, Mr. Green," Bruce protested.

Mr. Green made a sound of utmost contempt. "No Jap is *my* ally!"

It was hopeless trying to make Mr. Green concede a point. Bruce would not even have made the attempt if he had had anything better to do. But since he was entering the Armed Services next day, he was at loose ends. He had said all his good-byes; he had cleared up all his business; nothing remained for him to do now except report at the courthouse next morning.

"Now *that*," Mr. Green said, looking proudly upon the mounting blaze, "that's a *real* fire."

Though Bruce Berwyn was a sincere, if not devout Methodist, he had never felt himself called to the religious life. He had any number of firm opinions, which he set considerable store upon, but they were none of them characterized by unorthodoxy. He was neither very short nor very tall, very fat nor very thin; he had 20-20 vision and an IQ of 106. He did not wet his bed, nor did he have frequent and terrifying nightmares. He had, once, used narcotics (marijuana, nothing more than that), but he had not seen fit to mention this on the Selective Service questionnaire. There had never been any doubt in his mind, nor in the minds of those who knew him, that he would be classified 1-A, and so he had been.

The prospect of military service had been there, in Bruce's future, ever since he had been aware of having any future at all. Thus, he did not look upon it as an interruption in the natural course of his life, for it was a part of that natural course—almost, for the moment, its definition. After the Army he would find a good job and marry, have kids, buy a home, retire, and then just settle back and *enjoy* things. That was the way it was done; that was the way he would do it.

And besides—he owed it to his country. Citizens, as Bruce well knew, had responsibilities as well as rights, duties as well as privileges.

1-A

Service in the Army is a duty and a privilege. Each individual in this nation has the duty to contribute as much as he can to the well-being of the nation and its people. Military service is one form of such a contribution. From the oldest times, it has been considered a privilege to be permitted to bear arms in the defense of one's nation or people. This privilege is afforded only to those who are individuals of good standing and of good reputation.

from *The Soldier's Guide, Department of the Army Field Manual FM 21-13*

No one could gainsay that Bruce was an individual of good standing and reputation. Ergo, the Army.

Bruce, who had never flown before, was pleasantly surprised to find that he was to be taken to Fort Candler in an airplane. The officer who had sworn the draftees in at the courthouse did not accompany them on the plane, so that Bruce's first taste of Army life could not have been more agreeable.

The trip took only an hour and ten minutes, but in that time Bruce made good friends with four other inductees. They exchanged lighthearted anecdotes about the idiocies and hardships of Army life, but mainly about the idiocies. One fellow had had a brother in the Regular Army, a career man, who had been in a platoon that had been anxious to win the pennant that was awarded each week after inspection to the tidiest platoon. This platoon would scrub and polish and clean their rifles till very late on Friday night, but since all the other platoons did this too, their efforts went unrecognized. They had to do something uniquely neat, and this was the stratagem they eventually devised: each man emptied out a tube of toothpaste and filled it with quick-drying cement; when the cement was firm, he scraped the paint off, painted the tube with copper paint and polished it until it shone as brightly as the brass on his jacket's lapels. The platoon won the pennant the first week this was done, but by the next week all the other platoons in the Regiment had learned the same trick. This anecdote was reassuring to Bruce and the other draftees, for, among its many lessons, it showed that the Army was essentially a sort of game. One only had to learn the rules, which were, it is true, rather arbitrary, and all would be well. One only had to keep in step. If a person could maintain an attitude of cool detachment, the Army might even prove to be a source of amusement.

Even so, in dismounting from the plane one of the inductees who had been liveliest in the exchange of anecdotes was attacked by what seemed to be a hysterical fit, after which he fell unconscious. This had the effect of casting a pall over the whole reception ceremony.

The draftees were driven the rest of the way to Fort Candler in a bus, under the supervision of a fat, taciturn Master Sergeant. It was sunset. The Master Sergeant delivered his commands in an ordinary conversational tone and did not require them to stand at attention. They were all slightly disappointed, having expected to be bullied a bit at the first.

They were shown to a temporary barracks and told to assemble for mess in fifteen minutes. But when they had assembled, no one came by to take them to the mess hall, and since none of the new inductees knew where it was they had nothing to do but return, grumbling, to the cold barracks. They waited, sitting on the olive-drab bunks for a long long while for someone to realize that an error had been made, but no one ever came around and they had to go to bed hungry. Perhaps, one boy suggested, it was not an error at all.

> Being courageous does not mean that you won't be afraid at the same time. The true mark of courage is to overcome fear. Fear in battle is natural and most soldiers have been afraid, but they went ahead, even with shaking hands and pounding hearts. Actually, a little fear is helpful. Medical experts tell us that fear and anger sharpen the reflexes and lend strength, preparing you for extra efforts.
>
> from *FM 21-13*

The next morning Bruce found that he was, after all, in the Army now. He was awakened by a blast of incandescence and loud obscenity that tangled together, in those first struggling moments, into a single noxious knot; before he had quite unraveled it he was standing outside in the misty predawn, where the sergeant told them how they looked like a lot of puking babies. It made the sergeant sick to see them. He didn't understand why they didn't send him *men* any more. Well, the Army would *make* them into men, if it was possible, and how many of them thought it *was* possible?

There was general agreement that they all thought it was possible.

But the sergeant was deaf, and demanded to know again how many of them?

They *all* did!

The sergeant still couldn't hear them.

THEY ALL DID!

"You're goddamn right! And you'd better start shaping up as soldiers soon or ..." The sergeant left this threat hanging in the air. Or, it was implied, something terrible would become of them.

Then they were ordered to form into ranks, which sounded easy until they tried it. Each draftee had his own idea of how to come to attention and where to stand in relation to the others. The sergeant became ever more angry in correcting their ideas. Bruce, who as chance would have it, was standing in the first rank, became worried that the sergeant would single him out as the particular object of his satire. He sucked in his stomach and chin, puffed out his chest and stared dead ahead. The sergeant passed him by without seeming to notice him. Inwardly Bruce smiled, but he was careful to let no trace of it glimmer upon his outward man.

He was a soldier now, a GI.

As a soldier, you are always a fighting man. In combat you are prepared to give your life in defense of your country. This is the basis for the fighting man's code of conduct.

from *FM 21-13*

When the sergeant had concluded this first inspection there was a scarcely audible sigh that passed down the four ranks of the platoon. In answer the sergeant's glance flickered along the rows of faces, like an insect's flight, and seemed to alight on Bruce. But it was toward a soldier behind Bruce, in the second rank, that the sergeant made his way.

"Suck in that gut!" the sergeant screamed at his chosen victim.

"I'm trying, sir." Bruce recognized the scapegoat's voice, reedy with adolescence, as that of O'Brien, a chubby college dropout who appeared to be years too young for armed service.

"Don't talk to me, fartface, unless I tell you to!"

"No sir."

"And suck that gut in!"

There was a long silence, followed by the sound of the sergeant's fist sinking into the boy's soft gut. After the third such blow, Bruce risked a backward glance just as O'Brien, with a muffled cry, collapsed to the ground.

"The rest of you men had better shape up," the sergeant warned, as he left them still standing at attention.

"Help me up," O'Brien whined. None of them dared move. "Someone, please, help me. I think I've broken something."

Bruce could not help but despise such a fellow.

That day, after a breakfast for which appetite had been the sauce, the new soldiers assembled in a big auditorium where they took tests. Bruce felt that he had done pretty well on the tests, though there was one arithmetic problem he hadn't been entirely sure of. Afterward he asked two other inductees what they'd answered for that question, and each of them had given a different answer than his and than each other's.

That was all that happened on the first day, except that after evening mess it was discovered that three of the inductees were AWOL from the barracks already. It seemed quite unlikely that they had got outside Fort Candler, since a high wall of reinforced concrete surmounted with high-tension wires surrounded it and all exits were effectively guarded.

The next morning the sergeant told them they were all a bunch of fairies. They were soft—soft as the turds of a sick rabbit. But the Army was going to make them hard as nails. Wasn't it?

Yes, it was.

The sergeant thought a sparrow had farted.

Yes, it *was!*

Perhaps the sergeant should take up a collection to buy himself a hearing aid.

YES IT WAS!

Again the sergeant called them to attention and again he sought out O'Brien, who was standing today in the fourth rank. The sergeant quickly found a pretext to renew his attack. O'Brien fell to his knees after the second blow, but this time the sergeant ordered two other inductees to help him to his feet. Whimpering, O'Brien tried to crawl away. The sergeant caught hold of the collar of his cotton sportshirt and ripped it down the back dragging the boy to his feet. They stood then, as in a tableau, motionless, except for the trembling of O'Brien's thick legs. The sergeant drew back his fist. Anticipatory tears started to O'Brien's eyes, and he began pleading to be let off. "I'm hurt," he sobbed. "I'm hurt inside." Bruce and the rest of the inductees felt disgraced by his performance.

The sergeant hit him only once more, though solidly, then went off chuckling and shaking his head in mock dismay. O'Brien was still lying unconscious, face in the dirt, when the company marched off for the morning's processing.

They moved through the medical examination building as though on a conveyor belt, being swabbed and jabbed and thumped and stuck and probed in single file. Bruce managed not to wince when a Med Corps corporal stuck the needle in his thumb to obtain a blood sample. He had type "O" blood.

In the afternoon the inductees waited in line before a yellow building (all the buildings of Fort Candler were yellow, with green, shingled roofs), where, upon being admitted, they were, one by one, photographed and given their Armed Forces Identification Cards. Also, metal dogtags were made up for them, which they must always wear around their necks. The dogtags had a curious notch in one end, and one of the clerks explained that this was so that the tag would stay put in a corpse's mouth, the upper teeth being wedged into the notch. Bruce had never worn anything on a chain about his neck before, and he was conscious the rest of the day of the cold metal brushing clandestinely against his chest.

That night in the barracks Bruce overheard somebody say: "I thought it would be worse. You know?" And somebody else: "It will be."

On the third day they were issued their uniforms and equipment, first a duffel bag, then, though not necessarily in that order, fatigue pants, fatigue shirts, fatigue jackets, fatigue caps, boots, drawers, T-shirts, stockings, poncho, blankets, canteen and cup, canteen cover, entrenching tool, mess kit, helmet liner, field pack, gas mask, leather mittens with wool liners, and so on and so forth. They returned to the temporary barracks with their duffels bulging. They changed out of civilian clothes and into fatigues. Soon, except for gross differences of stature and coloring, each man was the mirror image of every other man. Only one element was wanting now for their metamorphosis to be complete.

On the previous day, after the identification cards had been drawn up, each man had been given seven dollars advance on his pay in order for him to purchase the few necessities that were not to be issued by the QM—toilet articles mostly—and for a haircut. The line outside the yellow barber shop was the longest and slowest-moving of any that Bruce had had to stand in, and this despite the obvious dispatch with which this operation was performed. Each draftee leaving the building would be rubbing his stubbly scalp ruefully or else he would have his fatigue cap pulled down to his ears.

Though there were three barbers working, the shop seemed curiously silent. The barbers were bored with their work, which consisted merely in using a clippers up the side of each head, then stripping off the top with another, slightly longer length of clippers. The linoleum was thick with the masses of fallen hair, like grain upon the threshing floor. Bruce was surprised at how hot the electric shears were. Because they were used almost continually, they never had a chance to cool.

Since Bruce had usually worn his hair in a crewcut during the summertime, the barbering did not strike him as an extraordinary indignity. Other draftees, however, seemed to feel their loss more deeply and would protest what they must have known was inevitable, or begged to have it left "just a little longer in front." One of the barbers would always humorously agree to leave it a little longer, though of course never doing so, but the other, a surly man in his sixties, became so annoyed with one of his customers (whose hair had come down quite over his ears) that he ran the shears over the crown of his head with such force that the shears, striking one of the natural prominences of his skull, made a cut two inches wide. A paste of blood and shorn-off hair spread down the boy's face, but upon cleansing, the wound proved, luckily, to be more symbolic than actual.

Bruce left the barber shop rubbing his head ruefully. Somehow a gobbet of the other draftee's blood had got onto his hands.

Returning to the barracks, he found his fellow soldiers in a great uproar. While they had been gone from the barracks, someone had entered the building and hanged himself from a stair railing. Some claimed it had been the Master Sergeant who had driven in from the airport with them their first night at Fort Candler; others, more reasonably, insisted it had been one of their own number, perhaps one of the three who had gone AWOL, or O'Brien (who, it later developed was in sickbay with internal injuries). Some, and Bruce among them, having arrived after the body had been taken away, doubted that such an incident had taken place. They were shown where one end of the rope that had been used was still knotted to the wooden railing.

Bruce went into the can to look at his new self in the mirror. Several other draftees were there for the same purpose, though they pretended to brush their teeth or shave. His face might have been any of the faces in the mirror.

> During most of your Army career, you will find yourself part of a team, and you will be expected to play your part in it. This is not all give and no take, for while you are giving strength to your outfit, it will be giving strength right back to you. The more you put in, the more you get out. This is one of the most important facts of Army life, and one of the hardest to put into words. More and more you will see that your outfit is not just a bunch of men, and that it is a sort of person in its own right. This is most true of regiments, battalions, and divisions.
>
> from *FM 21-13*

The next morning Bruce was assigned to a Basic Training company, "A" Company it was called, of which he would be a member for the next eight weeks. A sergeant from this company marched Bruce and the other newly-oriented soldiers from the Reception Center to "A" Company's barracks on the other side of the camp. It was fully half an hour's march. Their new barracks were identical in all particulars to their old barracks, and they were able to feel at home immediately.

At 1400 hours "A" Company was assembled in front of the high, reinforced concrete wall that enclosed Fort Candler (for they were now at the very periphery), and their captain, a certain Captain Best, addressed this speech to them:

"Hello there, men, and welcome to 'A' Company. I can see without looking twice that you've already been welcomed into the Army. Ha, ha. For most of you the Army will be a new experience. Whether you're going to enjoy it depends on you. It's a new way of life, and for some of you it will probably be difficult to adjust to at first. Remember that I'm always here to come to with your problems. There are also Protestant, Catholic, and Jewish chaplains at your service. The PX is open until ten in the evening.

"Now, some of you may be asking yourselves—what makes a good soldier? Well, I don't pretend to be any philosopher, ha, ha, but just offhand I'd say that a good soldier is loyal, courageous, self-controlled, and dead.

"What do I mean by loyal?

"By loyal I mean that a good soldier loves his country. He doesn't ask what his country can do for him, but what he can do for his country. In the last analysis, every other quality that makes up a good soldier is a consequence of this kind of *loyalty*.

"What do I mean by courageous?

"By courageous I mean that a good soldier is brave. He does his duty no matter what hazards arise. Courage keeps you going when you think you've reached the limit. You'll find, as you get to know the Army better, that there *are* no limits.

"What do I mean by self-controlled?

"By self-controlled I mean that a good soldier knows discipline. Discipline is the foundation of every army in the world. You've got to learn to take orders—fearlessly—without questioning them: that's self-control.

"Lastly, what do I mean by dead?

"In just a minute I'll show you what I mean by dead ... but first let me say, off the cuff, that I think this company is going to be the best goddamn company in Fort Candler, and that's saying something because Fort Candler is the best goddamn training camp in this man's Army, which I think you will agree is tops in the world. So, let's hear a cheer for 'A' Company!"

After Captain Best's speech, and after the cheer for "A" Company, a curious and very large vehicle, which moved on treads, lumbered up the gravel parade grounds where "A" Company was standing at attention. It was built on the general lines of a tank, but it was far too large and unwieldy to have gone into battle. It was quite the equal in length to one of the barracks. Moreover, it was not armor-plated, unless the bright orange plastic shell that encased it concealed armor-plate beneath. A flag floated from the central mast, and at regular intervals around the shell there were apertures from which the nozzles of small-caliber guns projected.

The captain raised his right arm, then brought it down sharply.

The guns within the orange shell commenced to fire upon the men of "A" company. They continued firing until all the men had been lying on the ground, either prostrate or supine, for some time. Then they ceased.

Bruce had got his in the gut.

> Each soldier must handle weapons even though he may never have handled them before entering the Army. Whether you are an old hand or a novice— *handle them with care. These weapons are made to kill.*
>
> from *FM 21-13*

"Now *that*," Captain Best said with satisfaction, "that is what I mean by dead."

Fun With Your New Head

Heads are so funny, and there are a thousand laughs in store for you in the new, improved HEAD. Everyone enjoys a talking HEAD, from young to old. Taste, see, smell, and "pain" with a HEAD. Experience every emotion known to the HEAD. And if you already have a HEAD, remember what the HEADS say: "Two HEADS are better than one!"

Everyone enjoys a talking HEAD. Every minute is different from the next minute in incredible thought-chaos of a HEAD. And every single HEAD is different!

HEADS are so funny. Listen to the limbless talking HEAD talk about "Freedom," "Death," "Beauty," and "God-Father." Make the HEAD fall in "Love" with you. Any HEAD can be made to "Love," if training manual instructions are carefully observed. Watch the worn-out HEAD die, talking, talking, talking till the moment it decays. Indeed, it is not an exaggeration to say HEADS are so funny.

Taste, see, smell, and "pain" with a HEAD. Every HEAD purchaser receives absolutely free a "Life-time" supply of "Food." Put "Food" in the HEAD's *Mouth*, then insert consensual Apparat into *Left Collarbone*. You will taste every molecule of the *Mouth's* "Food." Only those who have "eaten" with a *Mouth* can understand the incredible sensations of "Food."

Left Collarbone is likewise Input/Output source for *Right Eye* and *Left Eye*. See the strange little world of the *Right Eye*, looking at *you!* See through the *Left Eye* too! Then see through both the *Right Eye* and the *Left Eye* together. Every Exo-Expert HEAD has *two* eyes. Don't accept less!

Left Collarbone is likewise Input/Output source for *Nose*. Now, with the new, improved HEAD you can

Fun With Your New Head

experience the disconcerting primeval world of "Sex," as the center of the new HEAD's sex-tropic response is removed from obsolete and unsightly sacral area and redirected to the graceful *Nose*. Just one more reason why two HEADS are better than one!

Left Collarbone is likewise Input/Output source for "pain"-sensitive *Chin*. Throughout the galaxies there are creatures, often the most insignificant, that can experience the famous "Negative Pleasure," and now with a HEAD you can too! The new, improved HEAD is thirty per cent more sensitive to "pain," thanks to refinements in the *Chin*.

Left Collarbone is likewise Input/Output source and control center for *Adam's Apple*. Nothing is easier than to take over your HEAD's talking-function. Amuse your friends by talking through your own HEAD! What could be funnier than to talk to another HEAD that thinks *you* are just a HEAD too?

Everyone enjoys a talking HEAD, from young to old. Even more fun than talking-function of the HEAD is thought-function. Insert conpassional Apparat into *Right Collarbone*, and experience every emotion known to the HEAD. *You* will feel the HEAD's amazing "Love." *You* will be paralyzed with the HEAD's consuming "Fear" of pain and of its own inescapable death. *You* will hate your own self—perhaps the most exciting sensation of all.

HEADS are educational. Everyone should have his own HEAD to grow up with. HEADS provide an easy and stimulating introduction to basic concepts of xeno-language and xeno-culture. Each HEAD is given a thorough grounding in the astonishing cultural traditions of its autochthonous planet. A third of a lifetime is devoted to the education of every Exo-Export HEAD.

HEADS are perfectly safe for the young. The sharp, skeletal teeth are extracted from each HEAD's *Mouth* at the time of assembly and refitted with harmless, hydraulic pseudo-teeth.

Many designers consider HEADS to be an attractive addition to the decor of one's environment, especially in arrangements with contrasting xeno-flora and xeno-fauna. For the fashion-conscious HEADS are available now in a range of natural tints from brown through pink. When treated with new, special-formula *Fungi-X*, HEADS can also be cultivated in more agreeable colors, though fungifying processes will abbreviate markedly the lifetime of the HEADS so treated.

Everyone should have his own HEAD, and now everyone can! Thanks to the diminished *Chest* volume of the new, improved HEAD, the result of recent advances in biominiaturization, HEADS are cheaper than ever before. They eat less and take up less space too! So why don't you buy your new HEAD today?

Any HEAD you buy from Exo-Export is guaranteed to be the native handicraft of its autochthonous planet, where bioengineering has long been practiced by the wild-four-limbed progenitors and manufacturers of the HEADS.

There are a thousand laughs in store for you in the new, improved HEAD. Why don't you buy your new HEAD today? Why don't you buy your new HEAD today? Why don't you buy your new HEAD today?

Only 49.95 from Exo-Export Monopolies.

The City of Penetrating Light

It is, predominantly fun. It wasn't always that way but it is now. There seems to be no limit to it, this delight. Vistas are constantly opening up. Older generations would have a hard time understanding this, because of various psychological hang-ups, such as the Protestant Work Ethic and Freud. But we don't think about the past, not any more.

For instance, there are games, or else creative activity of various kinds, active and passive. Not to mention, of course, sex. A well-rounded life has many facets. I like to build model boats, and I know many people who have the same avocation and enjoy it very much. Once a year there is a model boat fair, and people come from hundreds of miles around to exhibit and exchange helpful tips. That's just one example.

Medical assistance is always available, so there is never a good reason to feel other than your best. That's my opinion. Everyone is entitled to his own opinion, or this wouldn't be a Democracy. We are not the servants of the state, but vice versa. There is always room for a free exchange of ideas. There are some people who wouldn't have fun unless they could wrangle when they wanted to, though I'm not one of them.

By the same token, I prefer individual to group sport. I am a good swimmer and I love to ski. There is no sensation quite like coming down a snowy slope with the wind in your face and the glare of the snow in your eyes, but it would take a better writer than me to convey an impression of it on paper.

Just looking at certain beautiful things can sometimes afford great satisfaction when you're in the mood for that sort of thing. Sometimes, for instance, it's more fun just to look at a person's body than to make love with them. Or mountains, deserts, the sea, grass, the grain of a piece of wood—almost anything, in fact. It's a question, predominantly, of being receptive.

Anyone who has ever been in love knows how hard it is to express just what it is about being in love that is so rewarding, though they will all agree, I'm sure, that it is one of life's most rewarding experiences. I have been in love a number of times, though I'm not in love today. It isn't a question entirely of sex, because it is possible to love someone without having sex. However, sex does add to the excitement of love—there can be no question of that. Once I loved a girl named Nina. We both liked to dance, and we went dancing a lot—at The Bridge, at The Metropolitan, at The City of Penetrating Light, anywhere that a really swinging band was playing. That was a wonderful time, which I will never forget. Nina had beautiful long blonde hair and made a lot of her own clothes, because she liked doing things like that. When we made love it was like being in heaven sometimes. Also, she had a terrific sense of humor, more than I do, which is why we eventually had to break up. That, anyhow, is my explanation.

But life goes on, and it's a mistake to regard one person as "necessary," the world being full of people. After Nina there was Carol, and after Carol, Sylvia. And for Nina, after me, there was Doug. Sometimes I think that life is like one of those games you learn in school, based on the concept of Permutations. But I'll have to leave my theory at that, as I am not really an intellectual. I appreciate it in other people, but I've always been able to recognize and accept my own limitations. If I couldn't, I'd probably be pretty unhappy, and I think everyone has an obligation to be as happy as he can be.

Right now I'm living with some friends of mine in a little old shack about a hundred yards from the beach. The weather is usually good so we manage to get in a lot of swimming and water-skiing and such, and even on those rare cloudy days there's something to do, looking up old friends and maybe getting a little stoned, catching a good program, or just some old-fashioned promiscuity. There are also pleasures that can be enjoyed in solitude. For instance, as I mentioned before, my boats.

But there are dangers in too much solitude, especially in unstructured activity. Sometimes Nina would sit around the place for days at a time not talking and not reading, not even looking at anything, and I'm fairly certain that at times like that she was depressed. Other times, of course, she was a whirlwind and you'd have a hard time keeping up with her. Or she'd talk. She could talk hours at a time, about anything you'd care to name. I probably owe most of my own conversational abilities to those evenings of talk with Nina.

Love has to be a give-and-take, and I've wondered sometimes what it was that I gave to Nina in exchange for all the things she gave to me. Sex, of course, but I believe there has to be more than that. She tried to explain it once, saying she felt with me sometimes as if she were in a Japanese garden, a stillness and a sense of quiet sufficiency. Her words. It doesn't seem like very much to me, but it must have meant something to her. Who knows? Anyhow, we had a great time together, while it lasted, and I guess that's the important thing.

Well, we'd been living together about three, maybe four weeks, when Nina met Doug. Doug was an intellectual, a fashion programmer for one of the really big outfits. I would have thought he was too old for her, but girls like Nina often prefer older men. We went a few places together, including a smorgasbord, but usually it was a lot tamer than that. I guess when you come down to it I'm a little too wild for that sort of thing. Anyhow, we just sort of drifted apart, though we never stopped being good friends. I took up with Carol, and Nina moved in with Doug, and we agreed it was the best thing. Neither of us felt any regrets, because it had been a wonderful thing while it lasted.

It looks like this has turned out to be a story about Nina, though I didn't think it would be when I started it. I've never written a story before, just letters sometimes. Maybe I'm turning into an intellectual myself in my old age.

The point I'm trying to make is this—that life is so full of beautiful experiences, and we should always be ready to accept them the way they come. And beauty isn't just some painting of it or the way things look underwater, but it's spread around everywhere. Sometimes there can even be too much of it and it can tear you up, but usually, I think, it's a wonderful feeling. So there's no excuse for not being happy and having a lot of fun.

Moondust, the Smell of Hay, and Dialectical Materialism

I

He was dying for Science.

This was, in fact, the very mausoleum of natural philosophy—all those great and long-ago intelligences metamorphosed here into rockpiles: Harpalus, Plato, Archimedes; Tycho, Longomontanus, Faraday; and, on the face turned away from Earth, a ghostly horde of his own countrymen—Kozyrev, Ezerski, Pavlov. And honor, therefore, to be the first, the very first, to join them thus corporeally, like Ganymede lifted living up to Olympus.

Nine minutes.

And what a wonderful thing it was, what an endless source of enlightenment, to know the exact color of the crater Ptolemaeus—gray—to measure more precisely than ever before the height of its ringwall—1.607 kilometres—to collect the samples of gray dust, to chip off chips of gray rock, to sample, to weigh, to analyze, adding always a little more data to the data there already was, expanding the horizons of the known world, today the moon, tomorrow Mars, on to the farthest stellar vanishing point where time lost itself in the triumph of entropy. Wonderful.

Ah, but there, like the skull in the cell of a Carthusian monk, was that dread word again: entropy. Why must that be the last word science had to say on every subject? What benefit to know that the universe, like man, was mortal? That some day the earth would have no more verdant landscapes than these of Ptolemaeus, that the sun would die, that there would be, at the end of all things, nothing, nothingness, mere death?

Death: no matter how many times he said the word his mind could not encompass it. Only the dead know what death is. And yet he would die in nine, no in seven and a half minutes. And neither he, Mikhail Andreievich, nor anyone knew why. A faulty control element, a small breakdown that is unreported, which then compounds itself. But that too was what was meant by entropy.

He walked on through the crater, away from the ship that had betrayed him, legs bowed wide in the bulky suit so that he looked like an injured soccer player leaving the field, careful not to let any drop spill from his cup of pain. He gathered up the last canister of dust and returned with the tray to the ship. Inside the helmet the communicator bleated for his attention. Six minutes. A little less than six minutes.

If I held my breath . . . he thought.

One by one he took the canisters from their tray and emptied them over the shoes of the puffy, bright-yellow suit. The moondust fell as straight and swift as a rock, with no trace of colloidal softness. An empty gesture. He faced the east where the crescent earth hung low on the horizon. Russia lay now within the dark, night-time area of the crescent.

And that was empty too, all space was empty and the earth only a rotating sphere in that void, the moon another, the sun and stars balls of hot gases. To think of it! To think that he would die because he had no more oxygen to feed his blood cells. To think . . .

But there was not time to think of everything. Soon, quite soon, he would have to stop thinking altogether.

The communicator continued to buzz.

Flies buzzing about a carcass. There could not be flies on the moon, though, since it lacked an atmosphere. There could not be life here, of any sort. All the lovely stories that could not be true because life could not exist on the moon. Even his own life, his own lovely story.

He realized that he was holding his breath, trying not to breathe. The dumb beast beneath his conscious mind still believed it would be saved. Poor brutish thing. Like his mother, kissing an icon with her last breath, while the intelligent gray eyes confessed that *they* knew there would not be another life. The lips believe, the eyes deny.

He tongued the communicator on. "Yes?" he said.

"Oh Mikhail! We were worried. We thought . . ." Tonia's pleasant contralto was still recognizable across the 240,000 miles vacuum.

"No, not yet."

"We've found out what was at the root of the problem. As Dmitri first insisted, the third fuel injection unit wasn't in synch with—"

"Please, Tonia. It can't help me to know *that*." His emphasis implied that there was, after all, something that it would help him to know.

There was a silence before Tonia spoke again. The change in her voice suggested that she had been crying. "We all think that you've been so gricky crack."

"So brave?" he asked, interpreting the static. "Is it brave to go on eating and drinking while there's food left? Is it brave to breathe? That's as brave as I've been."

"What did you say, Mikhail? We lost you for a minute."

"Nothing."

"Assya sends her love, Mikhail."

Four minutes.

"Send my love to Assya." He tongued off the communicator, thinking how like a kiss it was, and how unlike.

No, he was not dying for Science, for Science is not a good reason for dying.

II

He was dying for Love.

Had he not told himself, during that long-ago summer, that *now* he might die without regret, that anything more would be superfluity? And had she not been boundlessly beautiful, his Assya? The skin smooth and clear as the rind of an unflawed pear, the swift uncertain smile, the smell of hay in golden hair, the infinite perspectives of her gray eyes. Would not a single memory of Assya, the remembered warmth of that one summer, have supplied reasons enough for a lifetime?

But that is passed, he objected, *and of the past*.

Truly. As well try to hold still the turning world as keep loveliness, or love, from passing. It passes in years or in an evening, but it passes. There was no beauty, no nobility, no human worth that was not ephemeral. There is an entropy of the spirit to match the entropy of the world. Like her once-firm flesh, Assya's character had grown flabby with lack of exercise. For Assya, as for most people, death did not come at once, but by degrees. Love? No, there was none left now.

And yet the grass had been so green that summer. The sun had seemed to pour forth streams of liquid life. Lifting the bales of hay, working beside Assya in the heat, forgetting for the time being the pressure of the university, forgetting everything but their two bodies and the ambience between them, love, then time had been kindly and the black vault of the heavens only the canopy for their private delights. Oh yes, an idyll.

But long, long ago.

Now the fields where they had worked together would be wrapped in the ice-cocoon of winter, and, had the land not lain within the horns of the crescent, he might see it glisten as now the northern part of Europe glistened as it received the morning sun.

The earth died each year, but after a season of cold it rose to new life. His winter would not pass, but what of that? Could not he rest content with a single summer, a glint of the sunlight, one kiss? What would repetition add to what he already possessed?

Words. There was no consolation in words.

"Assyà," he whispered in a voice aching with regret and—though he would deny it—envy. For she would stay behind, and he would die.

A minute and a half.

The communicator was buzzing.

If only he could have gone out in a burst of glory, bright with a mothlike martyrdom, instead of lingering on a week, another week, to witness the diminution of all magnanimity, all love.

No, he was not dying for Love, for Love is not a good reason for dying.

III

He was dying for the State.

Science is impersonal. Love has a way of dying before lovers do. But there are ideals—he told himself—that possess the authority of the former without abandoning the essential humanity of the latter. He was, as any astronaut must be, something of a patriot—even in a small way a fanatic. He had been, since his eighteenth year, a Party member, which is not at all an easy nor a usual thing for a student carrying a curriculum top-heavy with math and physics.

He believed, with something like a religious fervor, in the future of his country, in its destiny. He was proud—as what Russian could not be proud?—of what had been done in five trifling decades, despite the forces that had always been arrayed against them, forces so great that even now, regarding the green globe swinging above the lunar horizon, he could not repress a small feeling of paranoia. Yet despite all this, despite all that *they* could do, it had been Russia, his own Russia, that had reached the moon first and put a man on it.

Though no one would ever know now that that man's name had been Mikhail Andreievich Karkhov. Only after his successful return to Earth was the news of the Soviet Union's great coup to have been made public. A failure would not be acknowledged, since it would not serve the national interest to make it public. And was not the national interest, in a larger sense, his own?

And yet he would like to have been known. A weakness.

Had not most of the martyrs of the Revolution, or of Stalingrad, died obscure deaths? Were their sacrifices less valuable because their names had been lost? He wanted to say, *no*, but his lips stayed firmly pressed together.

What if he *had* succeeded? What if he *had* become a hero? Would that have altered the fact that he must die, and that in the face of death nothing is glorious, nothing is proud, nothing is of worth but a little more life, a few seconds, another breath.

No, though he wanted to, he was not dying for the State.

IV

The oxygen was gone. He looked, uncomprehendingly, one last time at Earth, then, ignoring the buzzing of the communicator, he loosened the screws that held the faceplate of the helmet closed.

Then he was dead, and, though he did not know it, there is never a good reason for dying.

Thesis On Social Forms and Social Controls in the U.S.A.

MEMO TO THOMAS M. DISCH

This paper was submitted to me by a third-year Administrative Trainee, Jeremy Freihoff. All students in Sociology S12 (Atopics) are required to submit their own analyses of American Culture. I am forwarding Freihoff's paper for your consideration. Not that the paper represents an original contribution, but I thought it possible that Mr. Freihoff might be of some assistance to you in your present work. I say no more.

> M. Jackson Matrix
> Administrative Training Center
> New York City

Schizophrenia is the predominant characteristic of twenty-first century man, both socially and individually. It may be objected that schizophrenia is the basis of civilization as such, but only today has the principle of dissociation been consciously adapted to all social forms. The stability of modern society is the pragmatic sanction of its system of split-level living. A satirist of the twentieth century (George Orwell) proposed a dystopic society which had this three-fold motto: "WAR IS PEACE. IGNORANCE IS STRENGTH. FREEDOM IS SLAVERY." If, in retrospect, such maxims of "double-think" seem prophetic in an auspicious rather than a foreboding sense, it is a sign that man has profoundly altered his way of thinking.

If the lion has, at long last, lain down with the lamb, it is because in every sphere of action modern man has applied the law of opposites. Equal and opposite forces produce an equilibrium; conjunction breeds content. To the unwittingly wise adages of Orwell one need only add "LIFE IS DEATH" and it corollary "LOVE IS HATE" to summarize the operative values of modern society. Indeed, they serve this purpose so well, that I have found it convenient to organize my paper on this very basis.

FREEDOM IS SLAVERY

Quinquennial bondage (slavery every fifth year for all adult males between the ages of twenty-one to fifty-one) is the fundamental institution of atopic economy. Slavery in one form or another is typical of all large-scale economic activities. The pyramids are a monument to the power of the slave teams that built them; wage-slavery laid the foundations of the industrial advances of the nineteenth and twentieth centuries. The slavery of earliest times was relatively stable. Revolts were uncommon. But its eventual supersedence by capitalist forms of slavery was inevitable, for all men were not equally slaves. Under capitalism, the idea of slavery was denied while the practice of it was extended to every level of society.

"All men are (created) equal" (i.e., equally free) was a favorite platitude of the capitalist centuries. The corollary of this—that all men are equally slaves—was recognized only after the complete upheaval of society in 1978. The scope of this essay does not allow an account of the Restoration period or of the eventual success of the philosophy of Jeremy Lincoln, the founder of quinquennial bondage and many more of today's social usages.* Suffice it to say that without the genius of Jeremy Lincoln the world we know today would be a drastically different and, I am sure, a worse place.

At the age of twenty-two, all men are called to their first year of servitude. Until this time their education has been humanistically oriented, their artistic and rational

* An excellent history for this period is Marvin Lowry's *The Anarchy and Restoration in America*.

faculties cultivated, and the development of their erotic capacities encouraged. Ideally, they are totally unprepared for the demeaning circumstances that await them in a labor camp, for slavery is never discussed in polite society. In the preparatory schools all references to this subject are systematically suppressed, the student body itself being the most efficient agent of suppression. Those who are unequal to the strain are reserved for positions in the Administration, but such cases are relatively few and will be discussed later.

The shock of first arriving at a labor camp is of the highest importance in the development of a slave. Every detail of his new environment is calculated to disgust and terrify the draftee. He is stripped of any sign of individuality, cast in chains, and thrust into a dark cell, where his only contact with others is with his jailers, who, having but recently been in the same position themselves (and, of course, not really quit of it), are scrupulous in their attentions.

Catatonia or hysteria is not uncommon within the first week. After two weeks of wretched food, inhuman treatment, and, when necessary, the administration of hallucinogens, even the strongest are unequal to their situation. No one is released from solitary confinement until they have gone insane. There follows a period of basic training in which the draftees are conditioned to automatic obedience. They are usually susceptible to the most minimal suggestion in their exhausted condition; a peremptory command, reinforced with arbitrary cruelties, is more than sufficient to ensure an automatic response.

When the process of dehumanization has been completed, the draftee is completely without independent will or judgment. He is without a sense of compassion or even community with other slaves. All memory of past circumstances has been suppressed. The entire process of automatic obedience conditioning from induction to release into the labor force is achieved in not more than eight weeks. Failure is virtually unknown.

During this first period, the personality structure that has been twenty-one years forming is erased. Now, as the slave is trained in his work (which seldom, thanks to automation, requires great judgment or specialized skills, he begins to form a new personality suitable to his new environment. Slaves are, at once, aggressive and cringing, violent and lethargic; of brutal instincts and corrupt tastes. If such a body of men were to live in civil society, anarchy and bloodshed would soon be freemen's fate. Therefore slaves are quarantined in large dormitories adjacent to the factories and terminals where they work. Contact with the free population is reduced to a minimum. Those slaves whose work requires contact with freemen live in mortal terror of them, for all freemen possess the right of life and death over any slave—a right which no freeman scruples to exercise.

Within the closed society of dormitory and factory—or, as this unit is commonly called, the concentration camp— the disruptive tendencies natural to slavery are kept in check by the simple expedient of working the slaves to nearly constant exhaustion. One day a month, the Sabbath, is devoted to rest, drunkenness and supervised sport— usually knife fights. One of the outstanding problems of industrial management is the reduction of the Sabbath mortality rate.

Further than this, slaves have no vent for their murderous impulses. Their lack of any sense of fraternity precludes revolutionary efforts, and if this barrier were ever to be overcome by a community of despair, their conditioned fear of authority would lead sooner to catatonia than to an outrage. Their work absorbs all their energies, and as is well known, the most potent energies (for short periods of time) derive their force from hatred and fear. A year is the maximum time for which these energies can furnish a momentum greater than might be demanded of men operating at greatly reduced hours and for mere self-interest. It has been found that one man working these longer hours at greater tensions can accomplish the work of five men working under the conditions that obtained in industries of the late capitalist period. And that is the reason for *quin*quennial bondage.

After a year of slavery, the draftee is returned to civil society. The transition is effected by steadily decreasing sedation in a restful environment after an initial application of insulin and shock treatment. The freeman has only vague recollections of his term of slavery. When it is time for him to return to bondage, character transformation can be achieved within hours by similar methods. The "reborn" slave will have no sense of the time that has intervened. Complete schizophrenia has been achieved.

There is another reason for the institution of slavery than the purely economic. If this were not the case, the obligatory term of service could be reduced to shorter and shorter periods, as advances in automation were made. Technology, on the contrary, is concerned only with maximizing the national product, not with shortening hours or lightening the work. In fact, many jobs are made unnecessarily demanding if they do not naturally meet the minimal co-efficient of exhaustion. These co-efficients are calculated for three phsyical conditions (strong, average, and sick) at each of the six age levels.

Jeremy Lincoln, in his famous *Hysteria Economico*, has explained better than anyone else the spiritual meaning of quinquennial bondage. There he wrote: "Men must be slaves because they cannot sustain the burden of freedom relentlessly. The problem is not just the madmen who infect our governments, [This was written in 1971 during the height of the Anarchy. The old government was still officially recognized then. J.F.] who, whether their minions are drugged into happiness or kicked into submission, find pleasure only in the exercise of a demonic power. It is not the queen bee but the hive, the entire power structure that must be destroyed. Yet not heedless destruction, for this produces merely the mirror image of the past, but destruction and reconstruction aforethought.

"The principle of the hive need not be opposed to the principle of freedom. Man is many kinds of animal. The contradictions that any one man can encompass within himself can be encompassed by a whole society. Significantly, the converse is true: the absurdities of a whole society can be mirrored in the microcosm of a single man. This, then is our hope and our task. Only thus—by keeping the insanities of modern society within manageable bounds—can we hope for a world not of terror nor of robotic, lobotomized happiness, but one of social equity and individual freedom."

IGNORANCE IS STRENGTH

The ignorance of the two halves of the divided man of each other is the strength of atopic economy. The slave experiences none of the pleasures nor refinements of civil society and is so conditioned that he can imagine nothing better than the concentration camp. Correspondingly, freemen are comfortably ignorant of the conditions of slavery.

It has been argued (principally by the opponents of Jeremy Lincoln in the last decades of the twentieth century) that slavery is incompatible with freedom, that schizophrenia is a disease to be cured rather than a state of mind to be systematically encouraged, and that any job can be made pleasant and ennobling in a healthy society. It is true that the conditions of work could be improved in many factories, mines and farms, but such improvements are very costly. Efforts in this direction were begun for a short period following the second of the world wars. Certain classes of laborers prospered at the expense of the entire body of consumers. Even then the inequity of such a system was often remarked upon. Imagine the cooling system a coal mine would need to make these environments actually *pleasant!* There can be little doubt, in short, that some occupations (and these often the most basic in an industrial economy) are naturally offensive to the senses and the intellect of man. To require any single man to devote his life to such chores is to demand the sacrifice of his finest nature to the convenience of the community and the comfort of his fortunate brothers. On the other hand, if every member of society were to devote to these tasks six years in a lifetime of sixty-six, the work would be done without the exploitation of any group of society. Instead every citizen merely sacrifices a part of himself, and this "part" so thoroughly isolated from his consciousness that it need hardly be regarded as a sacrifice at all.

Not all the employments of man need to be divorced from the consciousness of freemen, for not all occupations are by nature enslaving. The simple household-type chores attendant on communal living are neither debilitating nor exhausting, if approached scientifically and apportioned fairly. Scarcely a utopia has ever been imagined in which these tasks were not performed in an equalitarian fashion. In modern atopic society, therefore, all freemen perform "services," which seldom require above an hour a day. The only exception to this is child-rearing, which remains largely the duty of the mother. Here, too, a system of

Thesis On Social Forms and Social Controls

schools, nurseries, and care centers organized at a community level, frees mothers from what might otherwise become a mechanical function.

Another type of work for which slavery is neither a necessary nor appropriate solution is the field of professional activity: music, engineering, architecture, teaching, medicine, scientific research, poetry, aeronautics, journalism, etc. Naturally in a society in which all men are free to pursue their natural tastes, there is no lack of men and women willing to perform these functions. In fact, almost all adults are engaged at one level or another in these and related pursuits. Moreover, since a freeman's subsistence is not related to his vocation, it is not uncommon to find people engaged in two or more unrelated professional activities.

Such variations in income as exist (they are small) depend upon professional excellence, though prestige and the admiration of one's equals are greater incentives. Greatly increased income can only be received by contracting for a term of servitude beyond that which is demanded by society. Since all men today are able to lead lives of comfortable leisure and since, moreover, too much slavery is detrimental to health, it is quite an uncommon practice.

The last class of work that needs to be considered is administration. Necessarily, this work could not be performed by freemen, who are quinquennially slaves, for continuity is essential to it. Administrators are not subject to quinquennial bondage for the further reason that their work requires more or less daily contact with slaves and the institution of slavery. No freeman could endure such awareness.

In return for this exemption administrators are required to work a thirty-hour week year after year. They are not so free as freemen nor so servile as slaves. Their work would not inspire devotion for its own sake as do the professional activities of freemen, and yet it often requires considerable training. Those children of freemen who cannot bear the anxieties that mount as they near their first period of servitude volunteer to be trained as administrators.

Positions and status in the Administration cannot be hereditary, for Administrators have no children. Sterilization is only one of many measures that prevent the formation of an elite in the Administration. (All Administrators are male.) Another measure limits their influence in policy-making. Questions of fundamental policy are decided not by the Administration but by an elective board of freemen, whose professional interests have qualified them for such a position. Their relation to the Administrators of a particular industry is analogous to the relationship between the trustees and the managers of an insurance company or bank in the twentieth century. (Such an analogy cannot be extended too far however: often, the trustees of one bank were the managers of another.)

The problem of *national* economic planning is handled in a variety of ways. Always the same division of functions is the managing principle. The forms employed are derived from the Constitution of the United States as it was before the addition of the Bill of Rights. (The Federal Government is, of course, concerned only with economic matters. Individual liberties are too numerous today to be defined.) The Electoral College is again a deliberative body with discretionary powers. What remains of elective democracy on the national level is a concession to tradition and convenience rather than an organic aspect of atopic society.

WAR IS PEACE

Europe has maintained twentieth-century social forms remarkably intact: Roman Catholicism, love and marriage, benevolent capitalism, and even, despite the ascendancy of Rome, some vestiges of nationalism.

Europe is a sort of museum of cultural history for America.* The great cities that remain there, Rome only excepted, and the mountain and seaside resorts are devoted to U.S. tourism. Under such circumstances it may at first seem odd that all U.S. citizens are under the Vatican's interdict. Europeans may not visit our shores, and (according to the Church's strictest theologians) may not even *converse* with an American. A Crusade against the

---

* Note: America—this word has a curious history. In earlier times it was sometimes used to distinguish the continent of the Americas from the territory of its leading power, the United States. The states that once constituted the Dominion of Canada, for instance, were once part of America but not of the U.S. Even then, however, this distinction was seldom made.

New Islam is recurrently being urged by minority statesmen.

Fortunately, the Papacy realizes that without U.S. exports and tourists, Europe would soon be bankrupt and starving, and it has reached a working compromise with the "Antichrist." That the United States has maintained a supply of nuclear weapons while Europe's technology has decayed ever since the Protestant exodus began in 1978 no doubt contributes to the stability of their mutual understanding.

Europe is a favored place for graduate and postgraduate studies in the humanities. It is estimated that one third of the U.S. population between the ages of twenty-two and twenty-six lives in Europe. Branches of Harvard, Yale and Princeton can be found in Florence, Rome, Paris, London and Stockholm. In the Forties the University presses had some problems with the reorganized Inquisition. The principle then defined by the Papacy—that of separate jurisdictions for Europeans and Americans—has since been applied to all criminal actions. As criminal law no longer exists for Americans, there have been objections by certain Europeans (mostly in the northern countries where Protestant influences still exist) that this is inequitable. Most of these critics resolve their problem by becoming United States citizens; those who do not are usually silenced by the Inquisition.

In the first years of the Restoration, the United States invited immigration from Europe. Within a decade the greater part of the Protestant population had crossed the ocean. The Papacy laid the ban of excommunication on any Catholics who went to the U.S., and this measure was largely successful. (It may be doubted, however, that without the steady emigration from the Northern countries and their colonization by the surplus populations of France and Italy, that the Papacy would have known such success.) The status quo is maintained on the continent by the Church's tacit acceptance of birth control; the population there has increased no more than one per cent in the last decade, and this increase is largely due to the small increments of land that are reclaimed steadily in Eastern Europe, devastated and rendered sterile during the Sino-Russian Wars of 1978-79.

A more detailed history of foreign relations is outside

the scope of this essay.* Needless to say, diplomacy has been immeasurably simplified by the mutual destruction of Russia and China in the Sino-Russian War, the ascendancy of the Papacy, throughout Europe, and the incorporation of the small American states of the twentieth century in the United States. The African Civil War is still continued by that unhappy and decimated people. Australia alone among modern nations is a popular democracy in the old style. Though officially in a state of war with America (since 1982) and the Papacy (since the Revocation of the Italian Constitution in 2013), it carries on trade relations with both powers. The nuclear stockpiles of the United States are the world's greatest guarantee of peace. Thus, the principle enunciated by Orwell shortly after Hiroshima—that war is peace—is still today the touchstone of international relations and for much the same reason.

LOVE IS HATE

Thus far we have considered only the impersonal aspects of atopic society. No economic or political system is inherently good; as long as the national product is produced, one system is as "good" as another. Goals may be set for the economy (e.g., a high standard of living, maximum utilization of resources, or rapid accumulation of capital goods), but these goals finally rest upon noneconomic valuations. The question is always: "What is the purpose of life?" A society's economic structure is its implicit answer to this question.

In the capitalist era, certain economic "laws" were thought to be operative independent of social goals. The Malthusian theory and modifications of it cast their pall over those centuries. Economics was, and in a sense still is, the dismal science. Surely quinquennial bondage recognizes certain of classical economics' unhappy facts—but it has transcended them.

Consider *1984*. Orwell envisaged a world in many respects the prototype of our own. He recognized the social value of schizophrenia, the slavery to the state inherent in

---

* For a detailed account of European history since 1974, the reader should consult Daphne Stassen's *History of Modern Europe*. For a statement of the orthodox European view, see Giovanni Papini's (Pope Calixtus V) *The Antichrist*.

any Communist society, and the stabilizing effects of a state of hostility among nations. He failed to see, however, that such a social structure is not incompatible with the highest order of personal freedom. Though probably a latent schizophrenic himself, he did not realize the full potentials of schizophrenia, nor did he really accept the identity of opposites. Freud himself, probably the strongest single influence of Jeremy Lincoln, was blind to the large-scale possibilities of his work. In his last years he wrote a book, *Civilization and Its Discontents,* that sounded the death knell of Western culture. With the advantage of hindsight it is perhaps fatuous to point out that—as Julia Knox-Wilson has put it—

> *Yesterday's Laments will be
> Tomorrow's Psalms in another Key.*

Civilization *does* put the screws on Eros. Structure deadens and absolute structure deadens absolutely. While life remains in the individual man he must combat the forces of order that society generates, just as the nature of the social order leads it to deny the desires of its individual members. On the individual level, this phenomenon is mirrored in the struggle between super-ego and id. In older societies, this struggle, if intensified beyond a certain point, would lead to dissociation or psychopathic behavior—at that time functional disorders. Today the split is regulated so that the two halves of the whole man are each capable of independent operation.

Slavery is highly structured and lends itself readily to exposition, but it is difficult to give, in a limited space, an accurate account of the society of freemen. A world without rules is made up of exceptions. Exceptional behavior is the natural province of literature, but aspects of it are bound to elude sociological investigation. The old complaint that everyday existence is dull and empty in atopic society (Australians are fond of this argument) is untrue. The difficulty of describing everyday occurrences in an orderly fashion would become apparent to such a critic if he were to try to summarize his own routine behavior in a way that did not seem "dull and empty." The following survey is, therefore, little more than an index of probabilities, a compendium of atopic maxims. A livelier picture is readily available in any number of modern novels.

Sexual satisfaction can be derived from an infinite variety of sources. Throughout history, however, sexual energies have been channeled through an ever-diminishing variety of outlets. Though taboos might vary from society to society, taboos of some kind were always present. The more civilized the society, the greater were the number of forbidden pleasures.

Today nothing is forbidden to a freeman. He may take his pleasure where he finds it. Atopic man is nothing other than Freud's polymorphous pervert.

Imagine how shocking the implications of this would be to even the relatively enlightened citizen of the twentieth century. Today a boy or girl can have sex (and, in fact, usually does) with either of his or her parents without the slightest feeling of guilt. During school years they will sleep variously with members of either sex and any race, participate in orgies, entertain fetishes, and indulge in the strictest chastity.

Such a radical change in behavior patterns has been attended by many changes in the physical environment. Many public institutions perform the services of a brothel or public pander. Since slaves perform most agricultural work, the old isolated rural life has become exceptional. The inefficient villages that served the farmers have disappeared. The largest part of the population, male and female, are transient. They live in public hotels and dormitories, appointed to suit the most various professional and sexual tastes. Many former office buildings, no longer needed for commercial purposes, have been refurbished to fill the increased demand for community living.

Though individual homes still exist, these are essentially matriarchal. Women, being exempted from quinquennial bondage are expected to look after their own children. That they do so willingly and happily is an argument for a true maternal "instinct"; women who will not raise their own children and those who are sterile are given a choice between entering the labor force or serving for a period as prostitutes.

Non-institutional child-raising produces a wide variety of childhood environments, which leads, in turn, to a variegated adult citizenry. This fact, plus an unprecedentedly rich mixture of racial stocks, is genetically and socially desirable. Freedom and progress are incompatible with uniformity.

As the child matures and discovers himself erotically and intellectually, he usually develops a predilection for genital gratification (in the Freudian sense). Not infrequently, he will establish a stable monogamous or polygamous relationship. Women tend to polygamy, and this has a salutary effect on the child's environment (not to speak of genital advantages). He is able to experience a variety of fathers. The usual ambivalence of young Oedipus toward the monogamous father, whom he both hates and admires, are directed toward distinct individuals. Ambivalence, once the chief impediment to full genital development, is eliminated. The conflict itself is, of course, not eliminated, but it *is* vastly simplified. This fact was observed in the twentieth century by Margaret Mead, a researcher in primitive cultures, but strangely it was not then considered as a remedy for the ills of Western Culture. One of the most important consequences of the sexual revolution of modern times is that growing up is no longer a process of rages and rebellions, frustrations and momentary release. It is, instead, experienced as a deepening capacity for pleasure and sensitive experience.

With Oedipal conflicts subdued and major economic discontents no longer existent, violence is uncommon in atopic society, although it has by no means vanished. Only murder is punishable by law. The murderer must pay to society a "wergeld" of years of labor equal to the years of bondage his victim still owed to the economy. Time is valued highly enough to make murder an exceptional occurrence. Minor expressions of violence occur, but no more significance is attached to a fist fight than to a passing affair: sexual satisfaction can be derived from an infinite variety of sources.

The freeman passing from youth to middle-age usually undergoes a noticeable character transformation. At this point sublimation seems to occur spontaneously. Men tend to limit their sexual life to monogamy, while their intellectual interests broaden and deepen. This does not mean that as youths they were wastrels or boors. On the contrary: symbolic activity is just as much a part of man's nature as sexual activity. Profligacy and culture are not alternatives. There is a psychic conservation of energy but it is between Eros and Thanatos, not between Eros and Apollo.

Casablanca

In the morning the man with the red fez always brought them coffee and toast on a tray. He would ask them how it goes, and Mrs. Richmond, who had some French, would say it goes well. The hotel always served the same kind of jam, plum jam. That eventually became so tiresome that Mrs. Richmond went out and bought their own jar of strawberry jam, but in a little while that was just as tiresome as the plum jam. Then they alternated, having plum jam one day, and strawberry jam the next. They wouldn't have taken their breakfasts in the hotel at all, except for the money it saved.

When, on the morning of their second Wednesday at the Belmonte, they came down to the lobby, there was no mail for them at the desk. "You can't really expect them to think of us here," Mrs. Richmond said in a piqued tone, for it had been her expectation.

"I suppose not," Fred agreed.

"I think I'm sick again. It was that funny stew we had last night. Didn't I tell you? Why don't *you* go out and get the newspaper this morning?"

So Fred went, by himself, to the newsstand on the corner. It had neither the *Times* nor the *Tribune*. There weren't even the usual papers from London. Fred went to the magazine store nearby the Marhaba, the big luxury hotel. On the way someone tried to sell him a gold watch. It seemed to Fred that everyone in Morocco was trying to sell gold watches.

The magazine store still had copies of the *Times* from last week. Fred had read those papers already. "Where is today's *Times?*" he asked loudly, in English.

The middle-aged man behind the counter shook his head sadly, either because he didn't understand Fred's question or because he didn't know the answer. He asked Fred how it goes.

"Byen," said Fred, without conviction, "byen."

The local French newspaper, *La Vigie Marocaine*, had black, portentous headlines, which Fred could not decipher. Fred spoke "four languages: English, Irish, Scottish, and American." With only those languages, he insisted, one could be understood anywhere in the free world.

At ten o'clock, Bulova watch time, Fred found himself, as though by chance, outside his favorite ice-cream parlor. Usually, when he was with his wife, he wasn't able to indulge his sweet tooth, because Mrs. Richmond, who had a delicate stomach, distrusted Moroccan dairy products, unless boiled.

The waiter smiled and said, "Good morning, Mister Richmon." Foreigners were never able to pronounce his name right for some reason.

Fred said, "Good morning."

"How are you?"

"I'm just fine, thank you."

"Good, good," the waiter said. Nevertheless, he looked saddened. He seemed to want to say something to Fred, but his English was very limited.

It was amazing, to Fred, that he had had to come halfway around the world to discover the best damned ice-cream sundaes he'd ever tasted. Instead of going to bars, the young men of the town went to ice-cream parlors, like this, just as they had in Fred's youth, in Iowa, during Prohibition. It had something to do, here in Casablanca, with the Moslem religion.

A ragged shoe shine boy came in and asked to shine Fred's shoes which were very well shined already. Fred looked out the plate-glass window to the travel agency across the street. The boy hissed *monsieur, monsieur,* until Fred would have been happy to kick him. The wisest policy was to ignore the beggars. They went away quicker if you just didn't look at them. The travel agency displayed a poster showing a pretty young blonde, rather like Doris Day, in a cowboy costume. It was a poster for Pan American airlines.

At last the shoe shine boy went away. Fred's face was flushed with stifled anger. His sparse white hair made the redness of the flesh seem all the brighter, like a winter sunset.

A grown man came into the ice-cream parlor with a bundle of newspapers, French newspapers. Despite his lack of French, Fred could understand the headlines. He bought a copy for twenty francs and went back to the hotel, leaving half the sundae uneaten.

The minute he was in the door, Mrs. Richmond cried out, "Isn't it terrible?" She had a copy of the paper already spread out on the bed. "It doesn't say *anything* about Cleveland."

Cleveland was where Nan, the Richmonds' married daughter lived. There was no point in wondering about their own home. It was in Florida, within fifty miles of the Cape, and they'd always known that if there were a war it would be one of the first places to go.

"The dirty reds!" Fred said, flushing. His wife began to cry. "Goddamn them to hell. What did the newspaper say? How did it start?"

"Do you suppose," Mrs. Richmond asked, "that Billy and Midge could be at Grandma Holt's farm?"

Fred paged through *La Vigie Marocaine* helplessly, looking for pictures. Except for the big cutout of a mushroom cloud on the front page and a stock picture in the second of the president in a cowboy hat, there were no photos. He tried to read the lead story but it made no sense.

Mrs. Richmond rushed out of the room, crying aloud.

Fred wanted to tear the paper into ribbons. To calm himself he poured a shot from the pint of bourbon he kept in the dresser. Then he went out into the hall and called through the locked door to the W.C.: "Well, I'll bet we knocked hell out of *them* at least."

This was of no comfort to Mrs. Richmond.

Only the day before Mrs. Richmond had written two letters—one to her granddaughter Midge, the other to Midge's mother, Nan. The letter to Midge read:

December 2

Dear Mademoiselle Holt,

Well, here we are in romantic Casablanca, where the old and the new come together. There are palm trees growing on the boulevard outside our hotel window and sometimes it seems that we never left Florida at all. In Marrakesh we bought presents for you and Billy, which you should get in time for Christmas if the mails are good. Wouldn't you like to know what's in those packages! But you'll just have to wait till Christmas! You should thank God every day, darling, that you live in America. If you could only see the poor Moroccan children, begging on the streets. They aren't able to go to school, and many of them don't even have shoes or warm clothes. And don't think it doesn't get cold here, even if it is Africa! You and Billy don't know how lucky you are!

On the train ride to Marrakesh we saw the farmers plowing their fields in *December*. Each plow has one donkey and one camel. That would probably be an interesting fact for you to tell your geography teacher in school.

Casablanca is wonderfully exciting, and I often wish that you and Billy were here to enjoy it with us. Someday, perhaps! Be good—remember it will be Christmas soon.

Your loving Grandmother,
"Grams"

The second letter, to Midge's mother, read as follows:
December 2. Mond. Afternoon

Dear Nan,

There's no use pretending any more with *you!* You saw it in my first letter—before I even knew my own feelings. Yes, Morocco has been a terrible disappointment. You wouldn't believe some of the things that have happened. For instance, it is almost impossible to mail a package out of this country! I will have to wait till we get to Spain, therefore, to send Billy and Midge their Xmas presents. Better not tell B & M that however!

Marrakesh was terrible. Fred and I got *lost* in the native quarter, and we thought we'd never escape! The filth is unbelievable, but if I talk about that it will only make me ill. After our experience on "the wrong side of the tracks" I wouldn't leave our hotel. Fred got very angry, and we took the train back to Casablanca the same night. At least there are decent restaurants in Casablanca. You can get a very satisfactory French-type dinner for about $1.00.

After all this you won't believe me when I tell you that we're going to stay here two more weeks. That's when the next boat leaves for Spain. Two more weeks!!! Fred says, take an airplane, but you know me. And I'll be d——ed if I'll take a trip on the local railroad with all our luggage, which is the only other way.

I've finished the one book I brought along, and now I have nothing to read but newspapers. They are printed up in Paris and have mostly the news from India and Angola, which I find too depressing, and the political news from Europe, which I can't ever keep up with. Who is Chancellor Zucker and what does he have to do with the war in India? I say, if people would just sit down and try to *understand* each other, most of the world's so-called problems would disappear. Well, that's my opinion, but I have to keep it to myself, or Fred gets an apoplexy. You know Fred! He says, drop a bomb on Red China and to H—— with it! Good old Fred!

I hope you and Dan are both fine and *dan*-dy, and I hope B & M are coming along in school. We were both excited to hear about Billy's A in geography. Fred says it's due to all the stories he's told Billy about our travels. Maybe he's right for once!

Love and kisses,
"Grams"

Fred had forgotten to mail these two letters yesterday afternoon, and now, after the news in the paper, it didn't seem worthwhile. The Holts, Nan and Dan and Billy and Midge, were all very probably dead.

"It's so strange," Mrs. Richmond observed at lunch at their restaurant. "I can't believe it really happened. Nothing has changed here. You'd think it would make more of a difference."

"Goddamned reds."

"Will you drink the rest of my wine? I'm too upset."

"What do you suppose we should do? Should we try and telephone to Nan?"

"Trans-*Atlantic*? Wouldn't a telegram do just as well?"

So, after lunch, they went to the telegraph office, which was in the main post office, and filled out a form. The message they finally agreed on was: IS EVERYONE WELL QUESTION WAS CLEVELAND HIT QUESTION RETURN REPLY REQUESTED. It cost eleven dollars to send off, one dollar a word. The post office wouldn't accept a traveler's check, so while Mrs. Richmond waited at the desk, Fred went across the street to the Bank of Morocco to cash it there.

The teller behind the grille looked at Fred's check doubtfully and asked to see his passport. He brought check and passport into an office at the back of the bank. Fred grew more and more peeved, as the time wore on and nothing was done. He was accustomed to being treated with respect, at least. The teller returned with a portly gentleman not much younger than Fred himself. He wore a striped suit with a flower in his buttonhole.

"Are you Mr. Richmond?" the older gentleman asked.

"Of course I am. Look at the picture in my passport."

"I'm sorry, Mr. Richmon, but we are not able to cash this check."

"What do you mean? I've cashed checks here before. Look I've noted it down: on November 28, forty dollars; on December 1, twenty dollars."

The man shook his head. "I'm sorry, Mr. Richmon, but we are not able to cash these checks."

"I'd like to see the manager."

"I'm sorry, Mr. Richmon, it is not possible for us to cash your checks. Thank you very much." He turned to go.

"I want to see the manager!" Everybody in the bank, the tellers and the other clients, were staring at Fred, who had turned quite red.

"I am the manager," said the man in the striped suit. "Good-bye, Mr. Richmon."

"These are American Express Travelers' Checks. They're good anywhere in the world!"

The manager returned to his office, and the teller began to wait on another customer. Fred returned to the post office.

"We'll have to return here later, darling," he explained to his wife. She didn't ask why, and he didn't want to tell her.

They bought food to bring back to the hotel, since Mrs. Richmond didn't feel up to dressing for dinner.

The manager of the hotel, a thin, nervous man who

wore wire-framed spectacles, was waiting at the desk to see them. Wordlessly he presented them a bill for the room.

Fred protested angrily. "We're paid up. We're paid until the twelfth of this month. What are you trying to pull?"

The manager smiled. He had gold teeth. He explained, in imperfect English, that this was the bill.

"Nous sommes payée," Mrs. Richmond explained pleasantly. Then, in a diplomatic whisper to her husband, "Show him the receipt."

The manager examined the receipt. *"Non, non, non,"* he said, shaking his head. He handed Fred, instead of his receipt, the new bill.

"I'll take that receipt back, thank you very much." The manager smiled and backed away from Fred. Fred acted without thinking. He grabbed the manager's wrist and pried the receipt out of his fingers. The manager shouted words at him in Arabic. Fred took the key for their room, 216, off its hook behind the desk. Then he took his wife by the elbow and led her up the stairs. The man with the red fez came running down the stairs to do the manager's bidding.

Once they were inside the room, Fred locked the door. He was trembling and short of breath. Mrs. Richmond made him sit down and sponged his fevered brow with cold water. Five minutes later, a little slip of paper slid in under the door. It was the bill.

"Look at this!" he exclaimed. "Forty dirham a day. Eight dollars! That son of a bitch." The regular per diem rate for the room was twenty dirham, and the Richmonds, by taking it for a fortnight, had bargained it down to fifteen.

"Now, Freddy!"

"That bastard!"

"It's probably some sort of misunderstanding."

"He saw that receipt, didn't he? He made out that receipt himself. *You* know why he's doing it. Because of what's happened. Now I won't be able to cash my travelers' checks here either. That son of a bitch!"

"Now, Freddy." She smoothed the ruffled strands of white hair with a wet sponge.

"Don't you now-Freddy me! I know what I'm going to do. I'm going to the American Consulate and register a complaint."

"That's a good idea, but not today, Freddy. Let's stay inside until tomorrow. We're both too tired and upset. Tomorrow we can go there together. Maybe they'll know something about Cleveland by then." Mrs. Richmond was prevented from giving further counsel by a new onset of her illness. She went out into the hall, but returned almost immediately. "The door into the toilet is padlocked," she said. Her eyes were wide with terror. She had just begun to understand what was happening.

That night, after a frugal dinner of olives, cheese sandwiches, and figs, Mrs. Richmond tried to look on the bright side. "Actually we're very lucky," she said, "to be here, instead of there, when it happened. At least, we're alive. We should thank God for being alive."

"If we'd of bombed them twenty years ago, we wouldn't be in this spot now. Didn't I say way back then that we should have bombed them?"

"Yes, darling. But there's no use crying over spilt milk. Try and look on the bright side, like I do."

"Goddamn dirty reds."

The bourbon was all gone. It was dark, and outside, across the square, a billboard advertising Olympic Blue cigarettes (*C'est mieux!*) winked on and off, as it had on all other nights of their visit to Casablanca. Nothing here seemed to have been affected by the momentous events across the ocean.

"We're out of envelopes," Mrs. Richmond complained. She had been trying to compose a letter to her daughter.

Fred was staring out the window, wondering what it had been like: had the sky been filled with planes? Were they still fighting on the ground in India and Angola? What did Florida look like now? He had always wanted to build a bomb shelter in their back yard in Florida, but his wife had been against it. Now it would be impossible to know which of them had been right.

"What time is it?" Mrs. Richmond asked, winding the alarm.

He looked at his watch, which was always right. "Eleven o'clock, Bulova watch time." It was an Accutron that his company, Iowa Mutual Life, had presented to him at retirement.

There was, in the direction of the waterfront, a din of shouting and clashing metal. As it grew louder, Fred could see the head of a ragged parade advancing up the boulevard. He pulled down the lath shutters over the windows till there was just a narrow slit to watch the parade through.

"They're burning something," he informed his wife. "Come see."

"I don't want to watch that sort of thing."

"Some kind of statue, or scarecrow. You can't tell who it's meant to be. Someone in a cowboy hat, looks like. I'll bet they're Commies."

When the mob of demonstrators reached the square over which the Belmonte Hotel looked, they turned to the left, toward the larger luxury hotels, the Marhaba and El Mansour. They were banging cymbals together and beating drums and blowing on loud horns that sounded like bagpipes. Instead of marching in rows, they did a sort of whirling, skipping dance step. Once they'd turned the corner, Fred couldn't see any more of them.

"I'll bet every beggar in town is out there, blowing his horn," Fred said sourly. "Every goddamn watch peddler and shoe shine boy in Casablanca."

"They sound very happy," Mrs. Richmond said. Then she began crying again.

The Richmonds slept together in the same bed that evening for the first time in several months. The noise of the demonstration continued, off and on, nearer or farther away, for several hours. This too set the evening apart from other evenings, for Casablanca was usually very quiet, surprisingly so, after ten o'clock at night.

The office of the American Consul seemed to have been bombed. The front door was broken off its hinges, and Fred entered, after some reluctance, to find all the downstairs rooms empty of furniture, the carpets torn away, the moldings pried from the walls. The files of the consulate had been emptied out and the contents burned in the center of the largest room.

Slogans in Arabic had been scrawled on the walls with the ashes.

Leaving the building, he discovered a piece of typing paper nailed to the deranged door. It read: "All Americans in Morocco, whether of tourist or resident status, are advised to leave the country until the present crisis is over. The Consul cannot guarantee the safety of those who choose to remain."

A shoe shine boy, his diseased scalp inadequately concealed by a dirty wool cap, tried to slip his box under Fred's foot.

"Go away, you! *Vamoose!* This is your fault. I know what happened last night. You and your kind did this. Red beggars!"

The boy smiled uncertainly at Fred and tried again to get his shoe on the box. *"Monsieur, monsieur,"* he hissed— or, perhaps, *"Merci, merci."*

By noonday the center of the town was aswarm with Americans. Fred hadn't realized there had been so many in Casablanca. What were they doing here? Where had they kept themselves hidden? Most of the Americans were on their way to the airport, their cars piled high with luggage. Some said they were bound for England, others for Germany. Spain, they claimed, wouldn't be safe, though it was probably safer than Morocco. They were brusque with Fred to the point of rudeness.

He returned to the hotel room, where Mrs. Richmond was waiting for him. They had agreed that one of them must always be in the room. As Fred went up the stairs the manager tried to hand him another bill. "I will call the police," he threatened. Fred was too angry to reply. He wanted to hit the man in the nose and stamp on his ridiculous spectacles. If he'd been five years younger he might have done so.

"They've cut off the water," Mrs. Richmond announced dramatically, after she'd admitted her husband to the room. "And the man with the red hat tried to get in, but I had the chain across the door, thank heaven. We can't wash or use the bidet. I don't know what will happen. I'm afraid."

She wouldn't listen to anything Fred said about the Consulate. "We've got to take a plane," he insisted. "To England. All the other Americans are going there. There was a sign on the door of the Con—"

"No, Fred. No, not a plane. You won't make me get into an airplane. I've gone twenty years without that, and I won't start now."

"But this is an emergency. We have to. Darling, be reasonable."

"I refuse to talk about it. And don't you shout at *me,*

Fred Richmond. We'll sail when the boat sails, and that's that! Now, let's be practical, shall we? The first thing that we have to do is for you to go out and buy some bottled water. Four bottles, and bread, and— No, you'll never remember everything. I'll write out a list."

But when Fred returned, four hours later, when it was growing dark, he had but a single bottle of soda, one loaf of hard bread, and a little box of pasteurized process cheese.

"It was all the money I had. They won't cash my checks. Not at the bank, not at the Marhaba, not anywhere." There were flecks of violet in his red, dirty face, and his voice was hoarse. He had been shouting hours long.

Mrs. Richmond used half the bottle of soda to wash off his face. Then she made sandwiches of cheese and strawberry jam, all the while maintaining a steady stream of conversation, on cheerful topics. She was afraid her husband would have a stroke.

On Thursday the twelfth, the day before their scheduled sailing, Fred went to the travel agency to find out what pier their ship had docked in. He was informed that the sailing had been canceled permanently. The ship, a Yugoslav freighter, had been in Norfolk on December 4. The agency politely refunded the price of the tickets—in American dollars.

"Couldn't you give me dirham instead?"

"But you paid in dollars, Mr. Richmond." The agent spoke with a fussy, overprecise accent that annoyed Fred more than an honest French accent. "You paid in American Express Travelers' checks."

"But I'd *rather* have dirham."

"That would be impossible."

"I'll give you one to one. How about that? One dirham for one dollar." He did not even become angry at being forced to make so unfair a suggestion. He had been through this same scene too many times—at banks, at stores, with people off the street.

"The government has forbidden us to trade in American money, Mr. Richmond. I am truly sorry that I cannot help you. If you would be interested to purchase an airplane ticket, however, I can accept money for that. If you have enough."

"You don't leave much choice, do you?" (He thought:

She will be furious.) "What will it cost for two tickets to London?"

The agent named a price. Fred flared up. "That's highway robbery! Why, that's more than the first-class to New York City!"

The agent smiled. "We have no flights scheduled to New York, sir."

Grimly, Fred signed away his travelers' checks to pay for the tickets. It took all his checks and all but fifty dollars of the refunded money. His wife, however, had her own bundle of American Express checks that hadn't been touched yet. He examined the tickets, which were printed in French. "What does this say here? When does it leave?"

"On the fourteenth. Saturday. At eight in the evening."

"You don't have anything tomorrow?"

"I'm sorry. You should be quite happy that we can sell you these tickets. If it weren't for the fact that our main office is in Paris, and that they've directed that Americans be given priority on all Pan Am flights, we wouldn't be able to."

"I see. The thing is this—I'm in rather a tight spot. Nobody, not even the banks, will take American money. This is our last night at the hotel, and if we have to stay over Friday night as well . . ."

"You might go to the airport waiting room, sir."

Fred took off his Accutron wrist watch. "In America this watch would cost $120 wholesale. You wouldn't be interested. . . ."

"I'm sorry, Mr. Richmond. I have a watch of my own."

Fred, with the tickets securely tucked into his passport case, went out through the thick glass door. He would have liked to have a sundae at the ice-cream parlor across the street, but he couldn't afford it. He couldn't afford anything unless he was able to sell his watch. They had lived the last week out of what he'd got for the alarm clock and the electric shaver. Now there was nothing left.

When Fred was at the corner, he heard someone calling his name. "Mr. Richmond. Mr. Richmond, sir." It was the agent. Shyly he held out a ten dirham note and three fives. Fred took the money and handed him the watch. The agent put Fred's Accutron on his wrist beside his old watch. He smiled and offered Fred his hand to shake. Fred walked away, ignoring the outstretched hand.

Five dollars, he thought over and over again, *five dollars*. He was too ashamed to return at once to the hotel.

Mrs. Richmond wasn't in the room. Instead the man in the red fez was engaged in packing all their clothes and toilet articles into the three suitcases. "Hey!" Fred shouted. "What do you think you're doing? Stop that!"

"You must pay your bill," the hotel manager, who stood back at a safe distance in the hallway, shrilled at him. "You must pay your bill or leave."

Fred tried to prevent the man in the red fez from packing the bags. He was furious with his wife for having gone off—to the W.C. probably—and left the hotel room unguarded.

"Where is my wife?" he demanded of the manager. "This is an outrage." He began to swear. The man in the red fez returned to packing the bags.

Fred made a determined effort to calm himself. He could not risk a stroke. After all, he reasoned with himself, whether they spent one or two nights in the airport waiting room wouldn't make that much difference. So he chased the man in the red fez away and finished the packing himself. When he was done, he rang for the porter, and the man in the red fez returned and helped him carry the bags downstairs. He waited in the dark lobby for his wife to return, using the largest of the suitcases for a stool. She had probably gone to "their" restaurant, some blocks away, where they were still allowed to use the W.C. The owner of the restaurant couldn't understand why they didn't take their meals there any more and didn't want to offend them, hoping perhaps, that they would come back.

While he waited, Fred occupied the time by trying to remember the name of the Englishman who had been a supper guest at their house in Florida three years before. It was a strange name that was not pronounced at all the way that it was spelled. At intervals he would go out into the street to try and catch a sight of his wife returning to the hotel. Whenever he tried to ask the manager where she had gone, the man would renew his shrill complaint. Fred became desperate. She was taking altogether too long. He telephoned the restaurant. The owner of the restaurant understood enough English to be able to tell him that she had not visited his W.C. all that day.

An hour or so after sunset, Fred found his way to the police station, a wretched stucco building inside the ancient medina, the non-European quarter. Americans were advised not to venture into the medina after dark.

"My wife is missing," he told one of the gray-uniformed men. "I think she may be the victim of a robbery."

The policeman replied brusquely in French.

"My wife," Fred repeated loudly, gesturing in a vague way.

The policeman turned to speak to his fellows. It was a piece of deliberate rudeness.

Fred took out his passport and waved it in the policeman's face. "This is my passport," he shouted. "My wife is missing. Doesn't somebody here speak English? Somebody *must* speak English. *Ing-lish!*"

The policeman shrugged and handed Fred back his passport.

"My wife!" Fred screamed hysterically. "Listen to me—my wife, my wife, my wife!"

The policeman, a scrawny, mustached man, grabbed Fred by the neck of his coat and led him forcibly into another room and down a long, unlighted corridor that smelled of urine. Fred didn't realize, until he had been thrust into the room that it was a cell. The door that closed behind him was made not of bars, but of sheet metal nailed over wood. There was no light in the room, no air. He screamed, he kicked at the door and pounded on it with his fists until he had cut a deep gash into the side of his palm. He stopped, to suck the blood, fearful of blood poisoning.

He could, when his eyes had adjusted to the darkness, see a little of the room about him. It was not much larger than Room 216 at the Belmonte, but it contained more people than Fred could count. They were heaped all along the walls, an indiscriminate tumble of rags and filth, old men and young men, a wretched assembly.

They stared at the American gentleman in astonishment.

The police released Fred in the morning, and he returned at once to the hotel, speaking to no one. He was angry but, even more, he was terrified.

His wife had not returned. The three suitcases, for a wonder, were still sitting where he had left them. The manager insisted that he leave the lobby, and Fred did not protest. The Richmonds' time at the hotel had expired, and Fred didn't have the money for another night, even at the old rate.

Outside, he did not know what to do. He stood on the curbside, trying to decide. His pants were wrinkled, and he feared (though he could not smell it himself) that he stank of the prison cell.

The traffic policeman in the center of the square began giving him funny looks. He was afraid of the policeman, afraid of being returned to the cell. He hailed a taxi and directed the driver to go to the airport.

"*Ou?*" the driver asked.

"The airport, the airport," he said testily. Cabbies, at least, could be expected to know English.

But where was his wife? Where was Betty?

When they arrived at the airport, the driver demanded fifteen dirhams, which was an outrageous price in Casablanca, where cabs are pleasantly cheap. Having not had the foresight to negotiate the price in advance, Fred had no choice but to pay the man what he asked.

The waiting room was filled with people, though few seemed to be Americans. The stench of the close air was almost as bad as it had been in the cell. There were no porters, and he could not move through the crowd, so he set the suitcases down just outside the entrance and seated himself on the largest bag.

A man in an olive-drab uniform with a black beret asked, in French, to see his passport. "*Votre passeport,*" he repeated patiently, until Fred had understood. He examined each page with a great show of suspicion, but eventually he handed it back.

"Do you speak English?" Fred asked him then. He thought, because of the different uniform, that he might not be one of the city police. He answered with a stream of coarse Arabic gabbling.

Perhaps, Fred told himself, *she will come out here to look for me*. But why, after all, should she? He should have remained outside the hotel.

He imagined himself safely in England, telling his story to the American Consul there. He imagined the international repercussions it would have. What had been the name of that Englishman he knew? He had lived in London. It began with *C* or *Ch*.

Casablanca

An attractive middle-aged woman sat down on the other end of his suitcase and began speaking in rapid French, making quick gestures, like karate chops, with her well-groomed hand. She was trying to explain something to him, but of course he couldn't understand her. She broke into tears. Fred couldn't even offer her his handkerchief, because it was dirty from last night.

"My wife," he tried to explain. "My—wife—is missing. My wife."

"Bee-yay," the woman said despairingly. "Vote bee-yay." She showed him a handful of dirham notes in large denominations.

"I wish I could understand what it is you want," he said.

She went away from him, as though she were angry, as though he had said something to insult her.

Fred felt someone tugging at his shoe. He remembered, with a start of terror waking in the cell, the old man tugging at his shoes, trying to steal them but not understanding, apparently, about the laces.

It was only, after all, a shoe shine boy. He had already begun to brush Fred's shoes, which were, he could see, rather dirty. He pushed the boy away.

He had to go back to the hotel to see if his wife had returned there, but he hadn't the money for another taxi and there was no one in the waiting room that he dared trust with the bags.

Yet he couldn't leave Casablanca without his wife. Could he? But if he did stay, what was he to do, if the police would not listen to him?

At about ten o'clock the waiting room grew quiet. All that day no planes had entered or left the airfield. Everyone here was waiting for tomorrow's plane to London. How were so many people, and so much luggage, to fit on one plane, even the largest jet? Did they all have tickets?

They slept anywhere, on the hard benches, on newspapers on the concrete floor, on the narrow window ledges. Fred was one of the luckiest, because he could sleep on his three suitcases.

When he woke the next morning, he found that his passport and the two tickets had been stolen from his breast pocket. He still had his billfold, because he had slept on his back. It contained nine dirham.

Christmas morning, Fred went out and treated himself to

an ice-cream sundae. Nobody seemed to be celebrating the holiday in Casablanca. Most of the shops in the ancient medina (where Fred had found a hotel room for three dirham a day) were open for business, while in the European quarter one couldn't tell if the stores were closed permanently or just for the day.

Going past the Belmonte, Fred stopped, as was his custom, to ask after his wife. The manager was very polite and said that nothing was known of Mrs. Richmond. The police had her description now.

Hoping to delay the moment when he sat down before the sundae, he walked to the post office and asked if there had been any answer to his telegram to the American Embassy in London. There had not.

When at last he did have his sundae it didn't seem quite as good as he had remembered. There was so little of it! He sat down for an hour with his empty dish, watching the drizzling rain. He was alone in the ice-cream parlor. The windows of the travel agency across the street were covered up by a heavy metal shutter, from which the yellow paint was flaking.

The waiter came and sat down at Fred's table. *"Il pleut, Monsieur Richmon. It rains. Il pleut."*

"Yes, it does," said Fred. "It rains. It falls. Fall-out."

But the waiter had very little English. "Merry Christmas," he said, *"Joyeux Noël.* Merry Christmas."

Fred agreed.

When the drizzle had cleared a bit, Fred strolled to the United Nations Plaza and found a bench under a palm tree that was dry. Despite the cold and damp, he didn't want to return to his cramped hotel room and spend the rest of the day sitting on the edge of his bed.

Fred was by no means alone in the plaza. A number of figures in heavy woolen djelabas, with hoods over their heads, stood or sat on benches, or strolled in circles on the gravel paths. The djelabas made ideal raincoats ... Fred had sold his own London Fog three days before for twenty dirham. He was getting better prices for his things now that he had learned to count in French.

The hardest lesson to learn (and he had not yet learned it) was to keep from thinking. When he could do that, he wouldn't become angry, or afraid.

At noon the whistle blew in the handsome tower at the end of the plaza, from the top of which one could see all of Casablanca in every direction. Fred took out the cheese sandwich from the pocket of his suit coat and ate it, a little bit at a time. Then he took out the chocolate bar with almonds. His mouth began to water.

A shoe shine boy scampered across the graveled circle and sat down in the damp at Fred's feet. He tried to lift Fred's foot and place it on his box.

"No," said Fred. "Go away."

"*Monsieur, monsieur,*" the boy insisted. Or, perhaps, "*Merci, merci.*"

Fred looked down guiltily at his shoes. They were very dirty. He hadn't had them shined in weeks.

The boy kept whistling those meaningless words at him. His gaze was fixed on Fred's chocolate bar. Fred pushed him away with the side of his foot. The boy grabbed for the candy. Fred struck him in the side of his head. The chocolate bar fell to the ground, not far from the boy's callused feet. The boy lay on his side, whimpering.

"You little sneak!" Fred shouted at him.

It was a clear-cut case of thievery. He was furious. He had a right to be furious. Standing up to his full height, his foot came down accidentally on the boy's rubbishy shoe shine box. The wood splintered.

The boy began to gabble at Fred in Arabic. He scurried forward on hands and knees to pick up the pieces of the box.

"You asked for this," Fred said. He kicked the boy in the ribs. The boy rolled with the blow, as though he were not unused to such treatment. "Little beggar! Thief!" Fred screamed.

He bent forward and tried to grasp a handhold in the boy's hair, but it was cut too close to his head, to prevent lice. Fred hit him again in the face, but now the boy was on his feet and running.

There was no use pursuing him, he was too fast, too fast.

Fred's face was violet and red, and his white hair, in need of a trim, straggled down over his flushed forehead. He had not noticed, while he was beating the boy, the group of Arabs, or Moslems, or whatever they were, that had gathered around him to watch. Fred could not read the expressions on their dark, wrinkly faces.

"Did you see that?" he asked loudly. "Did you see

what that little thief tried to do? Did you see him try to steal ... my candy bar?"

One of the men, in a long djelaba striped with brown, said something to Fred that sounded like so much gargling. Another, younger man, in European dress, struck Fred in the face. Fred teetered backward.

"Now see here!" He had no time to tell them he was an American citizen. The next blow caught him in the mouth, and he fell to the ground. Once he was lying on his back, the older men joined in in kicking him. Some kicked him in the ribs, others in his head, still others had to content themselves with his legs. Curiously, nobody went for his groin. The shoe shine boy watched from a distance, and when Fred was unconscious, came forward and removed his shoes. The young man who had first hit him removed his suit coat and his belt. Wisely, Fred had left his billfold behind at his hotel.

When he woke he was sitting on the bench again. A policeman was addressing him in Arabic. Fred shook his head uncomprehendingly. His back hurt dreadfully, from when he had fallen to the ground. The policeman addressed him in French. He shivered. Their kicks had not damaged him so much as he had expected. Except for the young man, they had worn slippers instead of shoes. His face experienced only a dull ache, but there was blood all down the front of his shirt, and his mouth tasted of blood. He was cold, very cold.

The policeman went away, shaking his head.

At just that moment Fred remembered the name of the Englishman who had had supper in his house in Florida. It was Cholmondeley, and it was pronounced *Chum-ly*. He was still unable to remember his London address.

Only when he tried to stand did he realize that his shoes were gone. The gravel hurt the tender soles of his bare feet. Fred was mortally certain that the shoe shine boy had stolen his shoes.

He sat back down on the bench with a groan. He hoped to hell he'd hurt the goddamn little son of a bitch. He hoped to hell he had. He grated his teeth together, wishing that he could get hold of him again. The little beggar. He'd kick him this time so that he'd remember it. The goddamn dirty little red beggar. He'd kick his face in.